THE SPIDER:
SLAVES OF THE BLACK MONARCH

THE **MASTER** OF **MEN** !

SPIDER®

SLAVES OF
THE BLACK MONARCH

By Grant Stockbridge

STEEGER BOOKS • 2021

.

CHAPTER 1
THE GOOD MUST DIE

THE HANDS of the big clock in Pennsylvania Station indicated ten minutes to four as Richard Wentworth helped Nita van Sloan down the broad steps from the Arcade, and headed for the gateway that led below to the platform from which the Atlantic City train would leave. A quick glance had told him that the gate was already open, the train waiting on the lower level. His keen blue eyes glinted with satisfaction.

He had timed the thing perfectly—even though doing so meant arriving at Nita's apartment nearly half an hour late. In the bustle of getting her bags in the taxi, and the excitement of making the train in time, there had been little chance for questions or explanations. Now if he could get her down to the train, located comfortably in her parlor-car seat....

Alertly, he surveyed the big station from the top of the flight of steps. Everything seemed as usual. There was nothing but the ordinary bustle of arriving passengers swarming up from the platform stairways, late arrivals running breathlessly to the open gates, other groups congregating at gateways that were still barred by steel grills. Hundreds of people, standing and chatting, stopping at the newsstands, patiently waiting to meet friends who would arrive at any minute. Absolutely normal appearing— and yet today his eyes probed swiftly, as if somewhere in this

THE SPIDER

The underworld was
intimidating justice with
cold-blooded ruthlessness.

hurrying throng he must find the key to the curious excitement that tingled his nerves with expectancy.

"As long as you will be delayed until tomorrow, I don't see why I have to leave town this afternoon," Nita protested, and her eyes searched his anxiously. "There—is danger here, Dick?"

Wentworth smiled reassuringly. "The Haleys expect us

tonight," he reminded her. "You can go to the party and make my excuses. I'll get away to join you at the earliest possible moment."

"A dull party that will be a perfect bore," Nita complained. "I don't need a vacation and a rest. Just because I have a bit of a cold is no reason to pack me off to Atlantic City—and by myself, at that." Her dark eyes studied his face searchingly; her gaze narrowed accusingly. "It seems to me, Mr. Wentworth, you're working very hard to get rid of me, and it wouldn't surprise me at all to learn that you planned this 'unavoidable delay' very carefully. I've half a mind to call the whole thing off right now." She took his arm, and, though she still smiled, her eyes were large with anxiety. "Oh, Dick, if there is danger—"

But they were already walking between the railings that led to the train gate, and, before she could finish her half-decided ultimatum, Wentworth was handing her bags to the parlor-car porter and ushering her into the vestibule. Solicitously, he settled her in her seat.

For a moment, she was close in his arms, her own around his broad shoulders as their lips met and clung together.

He was still there when the clanging of doors and the trainman's "All aboard!" told him that the last moment had arrived. Nita planted a final kiss on his lips and pushed him toward the door.

Wentworth glanced at his watch as he stepped out onto the platform and the train door banged shut behind him. Four o'clock. With a frown, he glanced overhead and started double-quick up the narrow flight of stairs to the main station. But, before he had covered a dozen steps, his hand tightened on the railing.

Bedlam had broken loose under the lofty dome of the station, ushered in by the staccato chattering of an over-loud typewriter!

Richard Wentworth had heard typewriters of that sort spelling out death too many times to mistake the sound. Even as the machine guns above finished their grim chant, his ears were prepared for the screams of agony, shrieks of terror, dying groans and hysterical babble that came in breath-taking volume after a split-second of appalled silence.

HE LEAPED up the last steps and dashed through the half-closed gateway, prepared for what he would find. One section of the vast station had been cleared, as if by magic, of its crowd. There remained only half a dozen specks of humanity, stretched flat upon the cement floor. A hatless man, with blood running down the side of his face, was on hands and knees, vainly pleading with the bloodied corpse of a young woman. A mother screamed hysterically as she rocked the limp body of a child in her arms. An elderly man crawled on his hands, like an animal with its back broken, inching his way in agony, only to slump in a pool of his own blood....

At one of the gateways, four bodies were huddled in a heap. One was the uniformed ticket-taker. Wentworth saw this as he sprang out into that cleared space that seemed to hold the awe-stricken onlookers back as if it were barred with high-voltage electric barriers. The deadly typewriter had sewed a bloody seam across the front of the guard's coat, just as it had almost cut the other three men in half.

Tight-lipped, Wentworth bent over them and looked into the glazed eyes, the death-distorted faces. One was very familiar. For two days it had been pictured in every newspaper in the city, while the news columns were filled with stenographic reports of the testimony of George Roeble, the State's chief witness in its case against Ownie Garlauf.

Cold-bloodedly, the State contended, Garlauf had waylaid a payroll messenger and his guard and pumped seven bullets into them—shot them down, savagely emptying his automatic into their twitching bodies. From the window of a near-by store, George Roeble had seen the entire hold-up so clearly that his identification of Garlauf was too definite to be shaken.

And for that identification Roeble had now paid with his life.

The other two, sprawled half on top of him, were detectives attached to the district attorney's staff—men assigned to guard Roeble and get him safely out of town before the trial was over and Garlauf's confederates could organize to avenge him.

As he stared down at that gruesome heap, Richard Wentworth's deep-set eyes burned with cold rage, his lean poker-face pale, tense. For years he had been no stranger to sudden death. As he matched wits and the incomparable accuracy of his sharp-shooting automatics with some of the worst killers the underworld had ever spawned, he had been accustomed to the swift administration of gang vengeance. But the utter brazenness of this atrocity, with its callous contempt for innocent human life, left him stunned.

That woman out there covering a little face with kisses while she tried to wipe away the blood matting in the youngster's tangled blond curls—that picture stabbed at his heart and crystallized the grim determination taking form within him.

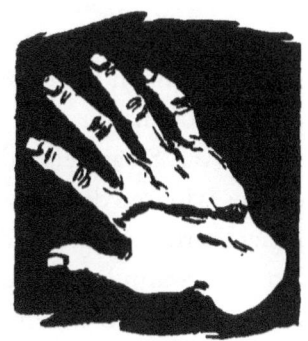

During the past few weeks, the criminal element of the greatest city in the world had been rising in what seemed open revolt. The underworld had gotten entirely out of hand, and the police had become as inept as children. Robbery, murder, holdup, cold-blooded killing—one on the heels of the other—and now this atrocious climax.

It was to fight conditions such as these that the grim crime crusader men knew as the Spider had come into existence, to mete out justice when Law and Order stood helpless, chained by criminal cunning. Never, in the Spider's experience, had the need been greater than now.

Richard Wentworth stared with filmed eyes at that grief-crazed mother—and the Spider made her a solemn promise of vengeance.

More than once, in the past few months, Wentworth had taken a trial balance of life's ledger and wondered whether it was worth while to go on with the career that had sent numberless powerful underworld lords to their graves and thwarted many a diabolically clever plot just as it seemed about to succeed—a career that had made the name of the Spider a symbol to conjure within the byways of crime. But much as he thrilled to the lust of battle, the matching of wits and pitting of strength, with life itself hanging in the balance, the way of peace and quiet had plenty to offer.

Nita van Sloan reminded him of that peace whenever her dark eyes looked deep into his and unveiled the longing always in her heart. Once the Spider was a thing of the past, Nita's open arms and warm lips waited for Richard Wentworth. The fullness of her love, constant joy of her companionship, home that he knew she desired more than anything else in the world—all these things weighed heavily on the side of retirement.

But while he stared at that tragic figure out there on the floor, fighting frantically as well-intentioned men tried to take the bloody little corpse out of her arms, the woman's face seemed to blur—and in its place he saw Nita's features, frozen into a mask of grief and horror!

Wentworth's hands clenched until the nails dug into his palms, and there was no further question in his mind. The way of peace was closed to him while monsters who could do a thing such as this roamed the city. Never could he give Nita these things she wanted so badly when he knew that, at any moment, the flaming muzzle of a sub-machine gun might snatch them away from her!

BY NOW the stunned crowd had recovered its senses. Assured that the menace was past, the onlookers were pressing in, mouths agape; and the station rang with the voices of men shouting frantic directions and orders that nobody obeyed. Through the clamor of the awed throng cut the shrill sound of a police whistle, echoed by the wail of sirens outside on the street.

At the stairways and at all doors blue-uniformed figures appeared simultaneously, unholstered revolvers leveled in steady hands. They were ready for anything.

"Stay where you are—all of you!" a sergeant bellowed through a megaphone. "Nobody leaves this station until he's okayed."

For a while, the place was a madhouse as men roared angry protests and women became hysterical. Then gradually the police produced a semblance of order, herding all who had been in the station to one side until they could be questioned. Wentworth was still standing over the piled-up bodies at the platform gateway when the crowd parted and made way for a handsome, florid-faced man in his late forties who strode forward with the brisk assurance of command.

Commissioner Kirkpatrick's gray eyes were narrowed in anger, and the muscles stood out on his jaws as he gazed down at the gruesome sight on the floor. Ambulance surgeons had given those bullet-ridden corpses no more than a perfunctory glance, turning to where their services might be of some use. The police had laid the bodies so that the faces were exposed, and Kirkpatrick saw their identities at once. His mouth worked as if he were about to speak, and then his eyes fell on Wentworth.

"My God, Dick—do things of this kind attract you like magnets?" he gasped as he reached to his side. His eyes clouded, an unfathomable expression filling them. "What are you doing here, anyway?" he asked. "How is it that you're always Johnny-on-the-spot when hell breaks loose?"

"I put Nita on the train for Atlantic City, a minute or two before they cut loose," Wentworth shrugged. "Check that if you want, Kirk. She's in the Deerwood parlor car—"

"And you just *happened* to be bringing her to the train in time to get a box-seat for this ghastly performance," the commissioner said skeptically. "That's the only reason you were here?"

"As a matter of fact, I was coming up the stairs from the platform when they opened up," Wentworth evaded. "It was all over by the time I got upstairs."

That was true, and he saw no reason for giving voice to the vague rumors, half-heard whispers, that had started him on this bloody trail and brought him to Penn Station at four o'clock that afternoon, prompting him to instigate the invitation that was even now speeding Nita van Sloan to Atlantic City. But the flash of suspicion had already died in Kirkpatrick's eyes, and in its place came a flood of worry and desperation.

"I'll be going around accusing myself, if this keeps up," he mumbled apologetically. "Stick around and come down to the office with me, will you Dick? I want to know what you saw—that'll be more than we can get from anyone else around here."

Which was true. Richard Wentworth had gone to a great deal of effort to establish a reputation as a non-professional crime-sleuth, a dilettante criminologist who played at the game when the spirit moved him. Commissioner Kirkpatrick had seen him in action on more than one occasion and had great respect for his capabilities.

Hand in hand with that respect ran a suspicion, at times amounting to a conviction, that the young clubman and adventurer he knew and liked as Richard Wentworth was the same person the underworld feared as the Spider—the same person whom he, as Police Commissioner of the City of New York, was sworn to trap and deliver over to justice for the unhallowed methods by which he carried on his guerilla warfare and enforced his judgments against those whom the Law, even in all its might, could not touch. That was what he suspected. At times, he hardly dared to probe his own mind to determine how close suspicion came to belief, and how near that might be to actual proof....

RICHARD WENTWORTH was a trained observer, but, as he sat in Kirkpatrick's office, there was little firsthand information he could supply. The show really had been over before he reached the blood-drenched stage.

"Damnable! Fiendish!" the commissioner gritted. "This outrage is the last straw! I know why it was staged—and if the devils get away with it we're licked, Dick. The police will be licked, and justice will be flat on its back. For weeks, we've been fighting the strangest threat I've faced in all my experience. It's just as if the crooks have united and decided that, if they can't lick our system, they'll upset it altogether.

"For weeks, the underworld has been shaking our courts until they're trembling at their very foundations! They've been threatening and killing witnesses, jurymen, prosecutors—even judges—until justice is practically paralyzed. What good is it for my men to arrest a crook or a killer? As fast as we bring them in, the courts turn them loose—even though everyone knows they're guilty as hell. They don't even try to escape arrest any more. They laugh at it—because they know that release awaits them.

"You see where that leads, Dick—to anarchy. No man or woman in this city will be safe—neither their property nor their lives. We've got to put a stop to it, or let the crooks take charge of the city. That's why we've been making a special effort to convict Ownie Garlauf. The murders he committed were unnecessary— sheer savagery. There's not the slightest question of his guilt, *and we've got to convict him!*

"The jury that's trying him is handpicked, men who have guts and realize the importance of their decision. We've taken every precaution to see that no threats have reached them. And now, at the last moment, this horrible slaughter is a deliberate attempt to intimidate them. But it will fail. I'll see to it that they don't hear a whisper of it until they have brought in their verdict! The case is expected to go to them the first thing in the morning— and I'll have cops a dozen deep around their rooms tonight!"

Perhaps those precautions would succeed, but, as Wentworth left the commissioner's office, he wondered. And again the half-veiled allusions he had heard over dingy bars, the fragmentary whispers caught as he passed close-headed groups of men who talked from the side of their mouths, came into his mind with new significance. Perhaps the Penn Station massacre had been staged simply as intimidation, but he could not escape the conviction that it was but the opening move in a game far more deliberate and deadly!

SLAVES OF THE BLACK MONARCH

IT WAS after two the next afternoon when word raced through the corridors of the Queens County Courthouse, in Long Island City, that the Garlauf jury had reached its verdict. They had been out less than an hour, but, with the damning evidence that had been piled up against the gangster, and the stern charge of the judge, it hardly seemed necessary for them to leave their box for the formality of voting—if their verdict was to be based on the case's merits.

Quickly, the crowd filed through the double doorway. Well up in front moved a shifty sort of individual with iron-gray hair and seedy-looking clothing. A perpetual scowl seemed stamped upon his face. That and the thick, metal-hooded glasses he wore were his only distinguishing characteristics, all that saved him from being a complete nonentity.

The sharp eyes of the attendant at the door probed at him, and turned away contemptuously to look for possible intruders more dangerous. At a glance, he classified Blinky McQuade as one of the hangers-on of the underworld; one of the petty crooks that constitute its fringe; a weakling satisfied to snatch up the crumbs left by his more successful and audacious brothers.

There were other sharp-eyed individuals in that courtroom who recognized McQuade, but their opinion of him was little more flattering than the attendant's. Blinky they knew vaguely as a broken-down safe-cracker, a Peterman who had bungled a job and almost blinded himself when the premature explosion left him lying unconscious for the police to gather in. They rubbed elbows with him in bars open only to those whose underworld identity was established, but even there he was accorded little more than toleration.

Blinky McQuade was obviously a harmless nobody. Nothing about his cringing bearing and careless, shabby appearance even faintly suggested the well-groomed, upstanding figure some of those same watchers knew as Richard Wentworth—which was exactly what Wentworth desired. On the day that he had dedicated his life to righting the wrongs the Law was unable to punish, a new personality rose, jinni-like from his makeup box—the Spider, an ugly, twisted, stooping figure with sallow complexion and discolored teeth, garbed in long black cape and floppy, wide-brimmed black hat—a vicious-looking creature well-calculated to strike superstitious terror into the hearts of wrong-doers. The Spider had done his work well—as many a luckless individual who had been saved from almost certain destruction could testify—but always his effectiveness was hampered by an inability to penetrate the crooked mazes where the police are taboo and where none but the crime's initiates are admitted.

To meet that situation and provide himself with another potent weapon in his relentless battle with the masters of crime, Wentworth had created the personality of Blinky McQuade—and immediately justified it by breaking up powerful evil forces. From that moment on, Blinky and his hide-out on Holian Alley became an established part of Wentworth's dual personality.

But if those in that crowded courtroom glanced briefly at Blinky McQuade and then turned away, the eyes behind those hooded glasses were far more observant. The seat into which he slumped was deliberately chosen so that he could watch a pretty young woman who had attracted his attention during the morning session.

White-faced, nervous, her handkerchief wadded into a little ball that dabbed at the corners of dry lips as she perched on the edge of the bench. Twice during the morning she had tried to say something, even half-risen from her seat before the judge's gavel rapped for order and an attendant threatened her with ejection. All during the intermission, she had remained there in her seat, and now her nervousness was close to hysteria as she stared anxiously at the door through which the jurymen must file.

Blinky McQuade noticed her every move, and other details, too. He observed the hard-faced killers who dotted the spectators' benches. They were men who would not have dared to enter a courtroom a few months ago and now sat there with brazen assurance—expectantly, waiting like theater patrons for the curtain to go up.

Sidewise, he noticed the painters at work on their scaffold against the wall of the building next door. All morning they had been splashing paint on that wall—but covering very little territory with it. True, the scaffold was lower now. It was exactly opposite the closed windows of the court as the painters fastened it in place and again picked up their brushes....

The painters were forgotten as the bailiff rapped for order and the judge took his seat on the bench. The hum of excitement died into breathless quiet when the jury-room door opened and the twelve men, who had been deliberating on the fate of Ownie Garlauf, filed into their box. Men with taut, pale faces—men who seemed afraid of what they had done but were desperately determined to stand by it.

The judge turned to them and started to speak—and, at that moment, the ashen-faced girl sprang to her feet.

"Oh, Phil!" she screamed. "You—"

But the attendant was ready for her. Even before the judge rapped for order, he yanked her from her seat, dragging her, protesting and pleading, to the rear of the chamber. And there she remained.

Now the jurymen had risen, and their foreman, a clean-cut looking businessman of about thirty, wet his lips.

"We," he announced clearly and firmly, "find the defendant, Owen Garlauf, guil—"

The last syllable of that word was drowned in a blast of noise that swept the courtroom with stunning suddenness. There came the shattering of glass, the deadly chatter of a sub-machine gun, the louder bark of an automatic, shrieks of terror, the mad uproar of overturned tables and benches as terrified people sought safety on the floor.

BLINKY McQUADE saw the courtroom window disintegrate and the jurymen mowed down like tenpins, slumping back in their chairs or sprawling half over the railing of their box. He saw Judge Andrews pitch forward in his chair, his head rolling off the desk-top like a melon as he fell to the floor. Two witnesses, who had testified against Garlauf, staggered to their feet and crumpled as that deadly automatic picked them out of the crowd. Two members of the district attorney's staff slumped over the counsel table and bathed their papers with their own blood.

For just a moment, Blinky saw one of the painters on the scaffold sweeping the room with a blazing sub-machine gun. The white painter's-cap was pulled low so that the fellow's face was obscured, but, through the strong, distance-lenses with which his hooded glasses were especially provided, Blinky McQuade caught a glimpse of the killer's right hand—marked with an unforgettable livid scar just above the knuckles....

Then the ghastly show was over. Miraculously, the painters and their scaffold dropped out of sight, and the courtroom became a seething madhouse of terror-maddened men and women.

Desperately, the attendants and the police rallied at the doors to prevent anyone from leaving. But, in the rush, the ashen-faced young woman who had been ejected, broke away from her captor. She fought her way down the packed aisle until she vaulted over the railing at the front of the court and ran to the bullet-shattered and death-laden jury box.

The body of the foreman had collapsed over the railing and slid out of the box in a sprawling heap on the floor. Frantically, she knelt beside it, lifting the blood-spattered head in her arms while the tears ran down her cheeks. Blinky McQuade was close behind her now, staring into that box which had suddenly become an enormous coffin for eleven twisted bodies.

"Oh, Phil," he heard her moan as she clutched the dead face to her breast, "I knew this would happen. I *knew* it, Phil, but I couldn't tell you—they wouldn't let me. They wouldn't listen to me. Oh, God, I should have run up here and *made* you listen—"

Gradually, the terrified crowd was being quieted and herded back into the seats while squads of bluecoats and detectives swarmed into the violated chambers of justice. They were all over, pushing the more curious back, scrutinizing faces suspiciously, weapons drawn to meet another attack should it come.

"What's that you say, girlie?" One of the detectives bent over the weeping girl. "What did you know about this? Who are you, anyway?"

The sound of his voice seemed to dry up her grief as terror surged through her. Stark fear flashed in her eyes and her lips snapped shut like the jaws of a trap.

"Who are you, d'yuh hear?" The plain-clothesman took hold of her shoulder, shook her.

"Peggy—Peggy Dunning," came in a barely audible whisper from her white lips. "He—he was my brother."

"Oh, so that's it!" Compassion tinged the man's tone but was immediately banished as he returned to the scent. "Well, how did you know this was gonna happen?"

For a moment, her frightened eyes were hard and defiant. Then tears welled up in them afresh.

"Oh, there has been so much killing!" she sobbed. "I knew that something would happen to Phil as soon as he was taken for this case—"

The detective grunted something unintelligible and turned away in disgust, but Blinky McQuade peered into the twitching face and knew that Peggy Dunning had lied deliberately. It was no mere uneasiness, no woman's intuition that had racked her all morning in the courtroom while she tried desperately to get word to her brother....

BLINKY STRAIGHTENED and suddenly turned. The vague sixth sense that seems to tell some people when they are under scrutiny warned him that hostile eyes were studying him, too. He glanced up to see Red Corbin, a well known newspaper feature writer, talking to a detective and nodding in his direction.

Before Blinky had time to move away, the detective covered the intervening space and grabbed him by the collar.

"What are *you* doing up here?" he demanded belligerently. "Who are you? How'd you get up here?"

"McQuade—Blinky McQuade," Blinky sullenly mumbled his identity. "Just come up to take a gander, o' course. Same as anybody else. No crime in that, is there?"

Corbin was whispering something in the detective's ear, but the officer looked doubtful. Suddenly, he grabbed Blinky's glasses and snatched them off, stood regarding the protesting gray-head who blinked helplessly into the night.

"All right, put 'em on," he growled, handing the glasses back, "but I got a good mind to pick you up on gen'ral principles. Keep your nose out o' things like this if you wanta keep out o' trouble." Then he turned to Corbin. "Just a nosey rabbit stickin' his snoot in when the shooting's all over," he dismissed Blinky McQuade.

Whatever it was that Red Corbin had tried to get the detective to do had failed, but his interference had sounded a warning alarm in Blinky McQuade's brain. Corbin, he remembered, had been right on hand at the Penn Station massacre. He had been snapping photographs almost before the bodies were still in death.

Could it be possible that he remembered seeing Wentworth there? That he had in some way half-probed Blinky McQuade's masquerade and, for that reason, had tried to have the detective unmask him? Corbin had established a reputation for his articles on crime and analyses which often cleared up a puzzling mystery far more conclusively than the police. His interference certainly had not been without reason, and Blinky decided that he would be a very good man to keep under surveillance.

By this time another judge had ascended the bench and declared the case of the State against Ownie Garlauf a mistrial. The prisoner was led back to his cell, and the court attendants and police quickly herded the spectators out of the courtroom. But, as he departed, Blinky McQuade took a last look at the white-sheeted bodies waiting for release by the medical examiner.

For a moment, he seemed to turn back his mind and again ran the film of memory before the lenses of his eyes. The deadly machine-gun hail was hosing the jury-box, toppling the judge from his bench, sweeping the attorneys from their table. *All but Martin Egelhart, the assistant district attorney in charge of the case.* Egelhart had been directly in the line of fire from that window. It seemed incredible that he could have escaped, but, at the very moment that the deadly clatter broke loose, he had thrown himself to one side and ducked to safety....

Most of the spectators filing out of that courtroom were

white-faced and stunned, but spotted among the crowd were those who grinned with poorly concealed satisfaction. Hard-faced citizens who winked knowingly at one another and bridled belligerently when an attendant hurried or jostled them. The underworld had struck again with cold-blooded ruthlessness, and its denizens were enjoying their triumph while they waited impatiently for the signal that would sweep aside the last barriers and turn them loose on a defenseless city!

CHAPTER 2
SIGN OF SCAR

KIRKPATRICK'S HOPE of stemming the ever-increasing tide of lawlessness, by convicting Ownie Garlauf, had failed. More than that, it had backfired. For the underworld knew well what precautions the police had taken to protect the jury, the unusual pressure brought to bear to secure a conviction in what had become a test case. By two bold coups, the criminal strategists, who were building up this empire of lawlessness, had swept aside all their careful preparations, snatched his man out of the shadow of the electric chair and opened the door of freedom to him. With the State's chief witness murdered, and the fate of the first jury fresh in their minds, no jury chosen to try Garlauf a second time would ever convict him.

Yes, the case that was to put an end to the growing threat of the underworld had entrenched its wily leader more securely than ever. Richard Wentworth, still in the identity of Blinky McQuade, saw ample evidence of that when he got out of the

Second Avenue elevated at Chatham Square, turning his footsteps eastward into the warren of congested tenement streets that is a city within itself.

News of the courtroom slaughter had spread through this human jungle like wildfire. On every side it was being discussed, and, in the bars and back rooms, where the small-time criminal element gathered, the excitement was at fever pitch.

"They slid down the ropes from the scaffold an' run out to the street," a weasel-visaged individual at one of the bars explained to two hulking thugs who listened stolidly. "Out at the end there's a car waitin' for them with the motor runnin', and they're off slick as a whistle—"

Dark eyes glinted with excitement.

"That's the way to handle 'em," one of his hearers endorsed. "Put the fear o' hell in 'em, an' they'll think a long while before they send a man to the hot-seat."

His companion nodded vigorous endorsement, thin lips curling back from stunted teeth as his moist palms clenched and unclenched. Even though these petty thieves had no connection with the campaign of intimidation now threatening the whole structure of Law and Order, they were waiting like jackals for that edifice to crumble. Then they could rush in and commit the

RICHARD
WENTWORTH •

outrages that they would not dare attempt while the threat of punishment yet hung over them.

Blinky's course through the crowded, refuse-littered streets was not aimless. He was making his way toward a combination bar-and-clubroom rendezvous where the middle class of crimedom had its headquarters—a resort where penitentiary graduates held their reunion. None who had not done bits behind bars were eligible for the select circle of Balmy's Bit House. Straight from Sing Sing and Dannemora, and dozens of other penal institutions from the Atlantic to the Pacific, Balmy's customers were recruited. They made his place headquarters until they disappeared again on another enforced vacation—or checked out for all time.

Blinky knew that eyes were watching him from across the street as he turned into the squalid hallway and climbed the rickety flight of stairs to the second floor. He knew that, the moment he pushed the button beside a door at the end of a short hallway, a door would slide closed behind him and pen him in a little vestibule from which there was no escape while he was given a careful scrutiny. But these formalities held no terrors for him. His identity was well established at Balmy's.

THE GRIMY, smoke-thick barroom was crowded when he shuffled in and took his place at the battered rail. Yet here the talk was more constrained, the air more furtive. These were men who knew what was going on—not men who only guessed. Three or four of the faces he recognized—faces that had been over there in Long Island City when that fury of death broke loose. And their being there was not accidental; they had been on hand only because they *knew* what was going to happen.

But it would be useless to question them. More than that, it probably would be fatal. Blinky had no such intention. His ears were alert to catch every whisper, as he waited and watched the door expectantly. Then his eyes behind the thick lenses kindled with satisfaction. The door had swung in to admit a mild-looking, elderly man with a half-apologetic air. For a moment, he looked around the room uncertainly, and then grinned as he spied Blinky.

"Hiya, Reef." Blinky nodded as the other squeezed in beside him at the bar. "Le's get that table over there in the corner. My dogs are givin' me hell today."

Reef Schneider was nothing loath, and his smile widened when he heard Blinky tell the waiter to bring two shots of Kentucky Gold. Balmy kept the best of liquors for those who could afford them, but likewise served a particularly atrocious brand of forked lightning for those not so particular—and the latter was Reef's enforced beverage when compelled to buy his own drinks.

"There ain't much money peddling Mary Warner these days," he had confided to Blinky. "Reefer's 've become kid stuff, and kids ain't got the cash. Snow—that's where the dough is in this game."

But even though he grew wistful when he contemplated the easy money to be made in dope-peddling, Blinky knew that the old fellow would never get past the marihuana-shoving stage. He was an old man, and he knew it. His nerve had slipped, and he cottoned to Blinky because he thought he recognized in him another old-timer who had known better days.

By the third drink, Schneider had reached the happy stage at which a discreet question might not arouse his suspicions.

"I met a feller last week in a place up on the Bowery," Blinky hazarded. "He give me an int'resting proposition, but we both had too many drinks, an' by the time we broke up I fergot to get his name. Just my damned luck. Sounded like easy money, an' I might've been able to cut you in on it. I'd sure like to find that guy—but I don't even know how to begin lookin' for him."

"Don't remember what he looked like?" Schneider was interested.

"Ordinary-lookin', far as I can remember." Blinky apparently tried hard to concentrate on the vanished one's appearance. " 'Bout the only thing I noticed unusual about him was a scar across the back of his right hand. Sorta looked as if someone had laid it wide open with a knife about an inch above the knuckles. That's not much to go on—"

But apparently it was. Reef Schneider was making an effort to remember, also; then he was nodding his head confidently. "I've seen that gent," he said, "an' I know where to get hold of him. I'll look him up tonight and let you know tomorrow. If I locate him for you, maybe we c'n make a deal. S'pose I meet you here tomorrow 'bout noon?"

Reef Schneider knew the man with the scarred hand who had wiped out a whole jury! First crack out of the box, Blinky had struck the killer's trail. Once he got hold of the scarred-handed murderer, Blinky was confident that the Spider would find ways of making the fellow talk and compelling him to lead the way to the master-mind behind this incredible assault against society. But he could not depend entirely on Schneider. Another lead was open to Blinky which he could not afford to neglect....

FROM THE Bit House, Blinky McQuade walked toward the river until he came to a sheet-iron garage, one of several dozen crowded together at the rear of an empty factory. He unlocked the battered doors, stepped inside. Then he climbed into a second-hand coach model wholly unimpressive—unless the observer had lifted the hood and examined the high-powered, perfectly tuned motor nestled there, always ready to perform excellent service. Blinky lifted the back seat and swung the side-walls back, uncovering a carefully arranged wardrobe and a makeup kit replete with those plastic materials, pigments and cheek-plates necessary to transform him into the ugly, snarling Spider.

When the doors of the garage were pushed wide, and the car backed out into the narrow alley, it was Richard Wentworth who sat at the wheel. The task he was about to undertake was a bit out of Blinky McQuade's line. In fact, as he drove uptown to the Queensborough Bridge, he wondered if even Richard Wentworth at his suavest would be able to accomplish it.

From the telephone directory he had learned that Philip Dunning, murdered foreman of the ill-fated Garlauf jury, lived on 85th Road, in Richmond Hill. An anonymous phone call had assured him that Peggy, the dead man's sister, was there at the house. Evidently, the police had not bothered to question her after she left the courtroom. But Wentworth was certain that she had information of vital importance.

The shades were drawn and the windows of the lower floor of the two-story building alight, when he drew up at the curb. Peggy Dunning answered the door, herself. She regarded him questioningly through swollen, red-rimed eyes.

"Good evening, Miss Dunning," he bowed. "Allow me to introduce myself. I am Richard Wentworth. I was in court this afternoon, and there are a few points I would like to have you clear up for me."

Her eyes filled with terror and she reached out as if to close the door. But Wentworth was already halfway through it.

"I am a deputy commissioner of police," he assured her as he flashed the card which Stanley Kirkpatrick had once given him in a moment of weakness. But it is doubtful whether the pasteboard impressed the girl so much as his compelling tone and aura of mental and physical power which he exuded. "You mentioned something about knowing what would happen to your brother—and I am convinced that you meant just that. I am convinced that you had some warning, some tangible reason, to expect violence, which you have not mentioned to the police.

"Of course, I understand your reluctance to talk, in view of what you have already suffered. That is why I have come here to your home, to chat with you quietly. Nobody else will know what you may tell me. Surely, you understand the enormity of the criminal organization we are fighting. You realize what it will mean if this thing is not uncovered and rooted out before it has a chance to grow any stronger.

"We cannot bring your brother back to life, Miss Dunning. But we can save other innocent men from meeting his fate. You have it in your power to save them, if you will be frank with me."

SHE BACKED away from him, half-leading him into a little side-parlor that was a sort of reception-room. She was still undecided as she stood with her hands on the back of a high chair. Yet she wavered. Some of the terror had ebbed from her eyes and her firm little chin was out-thrust. She was on the verge of talking—but at that moment a tall, rangy-looking young man, with a shock of unruly, sandy-colored hair stepped into the room. His blue eyes snapped angrily, and glowing crimson spots crept into his high-boned cheeks.

"Not a word, Peggy," he snapped. "Don't tell him a thing. You know what I warned you."

"Mr. Wentworth, this is Edward Morgan, my fiancé," the girl introduced them uncertainly. "Mr. Wentworth is from the police, Ed." She was very hesitant.

"So what?" Ed Morgan snapped. "What have the police done for us? Set Phil up on a pedestal so that he could be shot down, that's all. If you start talking, the same thing will happen to you. They won't protect you any better than they protected him."

He wheeled, and faced Wentworth.

"We haven't anything to tell the police, Mr. Wentworth," he said bitterly. "All we want is to be left alone. We've had trouble enough already, and we're not looking for any more—"

"What I had in mind meant no trouble for Miss Dunning," Wentworth interrupted the impetuous flow. "Anything she cares to tell me will be strictly confidential. She owes it to her brother to come forward with any information that may help track down the killers."

"Don't worry," young Morgan flared. "They'll be tracked down all right. Phil Dunning was my best friend—and I'm not letting any cheap, bulldozing gangsters get away with murdering him. I'll see that he's avenged, but I'll handle it myself, without the help of the police—or even your private cooperation, Mr. Wentworth. There is nothing Peggy can tell you."

His breath was panting, big hands knotted into white-knuckled fists as if he wanted nothing more than to come to grips with the cold-blooded killers of his friend. Wentworth realized that there was no use arguing with him. If anything were to be accomplished, it would have to be through Peggy Dunning.

"I understand how Mr. Morgan feels," he tried once more to influence her. "But this is a very dangerous situation in which he wants to take a hand. The moment the men who killed your brother suspect that someone is trying to avenge him, his life will hang by a hair. You saw today how utterly ruthless they can be."

"Oh!" the girl gasped, and her eyes turned fearfully to young Morgan.

But he saw through Wentworth's strategy. "It's no use, Wentworth. You can't scare anything out of Peggy. She's not talking—and that's final."

"Have it your way," Wentworth turned to the door. "I've warned you; that's all I can do." As if on second thought, he stopped, took out his card case, fingered an engraved card from it and handed it to the girl. "Just in case you change your mind—or if you should have anything you want to tell me—there is my address and telephone number."

Morgan's suspicious eyes bored into Wentworth's back, as he went out the door and climbed into his car. A well meaning youngster, Wentworth sized up Peggy's fiancé, but a regular bull in the china shop. Unless his tongue cooled, or somebody took him in hand, he was headed straight for trouble that could have but one end.

Richard Wentworth had failed. Blinky McQuade would not

even get past hotheaded young Morgan for an interview with the girl. Now that put the thing squarely up to the Spider....

IT WAS two hours later when Wentworth's car rolled slowly down 85th Road, but this time he drew up to the curb half a block away from the Dunning home. When the door opened, a twisted, stooping figure leaped out and scuttled into the shadow of a tall hedge that edged the sidewalk. Several cars were parked in front of the building, the Spider saw at once—and in the same moment the hackles at the nape of his neck began to rise.

Something was wrong up there—perilously wrong. Already, his keen eyes had picked out that shadowy figure on guard at the edge of the walk, peering up and down the street so warily. A lookout—which meant there were others inside who risked no chance of being interrupted!

Warily, the Spider crept forward, clinging to the shadow of the hedge until before the Dunning property. Now the lights were turned on upstairs as well as down. One of those cars belonged to an undertaker, he noticed. But morticians do not leave sentinels posted outside the buildings in which they work—and certainly not ratty-looking sentinels such as the young thug crouched there beneath a tree, hat pulled low over eyes, hand thrust into topcoat pocket.

The Spider's fingers dug into the soft earth, scooped out a handful and wadded it into a ball. Noiselessly, he tossed it over the hedge so that it dropped into a clump of shrubbery near the Dunning porch.

Like a snake, the lookout whirled. The hand that darted fang-like from his pocket clutched a ready automatic. But before he could fire it, something leaped up out of the night, pounced on his back. Steel fingers clamped on his gun-wrist, twisting it so that tongues of fire shot up through his arm. His fingers went numb. Under his jaw a bar, inflexible as iron, tightened, smashing his throat back into his neck, forcing his head backward. He tried to scream, but the sound was only a gurgle in his constricting throat.

For just a moment, he caught a glimpse of the incredible face, lined and hideous as a witch's, that scowled down at him from beneath a wide black hat—and then the world seemed to explode inside his skull!

The Spider held the limp figure at arm's length, while he slipped his hands through the fellow's clothes and removed another gun. Then he dropped the thug behind the tree. Picking up the automatic that had fallen from the inert fingers, he tossed it and its mate into the bushes. The Spider's imprint was on his forehead.

Noiselessly, he cat-footed across the cement path and up the stoop. All seemed to be quiet inside the house, as he crouched close against the iron-grilled double-doors—all except for the sob that abruptly snapped off short in terror. Through the almost transparent curtain that draped the length of the glass, he could make out the reception-hall, the arch to the living-room at one side—and the broad back of a short, stocky figure just stepping through it, a soft hat pulled low over his eyes.

From his pocket the Spider quickly took a small ring of skeleton keys. Experimentally, he slipped one into the lock. Another—and the mechanism yielded noiselessly. The door opened on well-oiled hinges—and a puff of breeze wafted through and fluttered the light drapes at the side of the archway!

Before the stocky man started his pivot, the cold muzzle of an automatic jammed into his back.

"Hold it!" the Spider snapped to another thug who stood across the room with guns trained on two white-coated morticians who were backed, trembling, against a wall. "Drop those guns or I'll drill you!"

Fascinated, the second thug stared, color ebbing from his face as if the morticians were already draining the blood from his body. His hands became weak, trembling things and the pistols dropped unheeded from them. His eyes were glued, not on the deadly muzzle that covered him but at the face snarling beneath that floppy hat.

"Gee-e-z!" he croaked as if pronouncing his own death sentence. "The Spider!"

"Yes, you dirty rat—the Spider!" Wentworth gritted. Only now did he realize the beastly thing these heartless devils had done.

STRETCHED OUT on a portable wooden table was the body of Philip Dunning, the blood half drained from his veins. These thugs had broken into the house and overpowered the scared morticians in the midst of their task. Then, while one of them had kept the undertakers covered, the other had searched the house and rounded up Peggy, deliberately forcing her back to this room where she must witness the macabre finale!

His finger tightened on the trigger of his automatic. It took every ounce of his will-power to keep from sending a leaden slug through the cringing neck backed up against it. An inhuman devil like this had little right to live.

The man stood there as if paralyzed, not moving a muscle for fear it would bring the bullet that he could already feel tearing through his flesh. His automatic was still trained on Peggy, still clutched in fingers now rigid as those of a statue—*a statue with a livid scar across the back of its right hand!*

The Spider stared at that damning scar, and his face hardened. Not content with murdering Dunning, this fiendish killer stood there and gloated over his victim, compelling the dead man's sister to witness his triumph!

"Drop that gun and turn around!" The Spider bit his words off like cold steel, the automatic jabbing deeper into the thick neck. But in the same moment he caught the sound of footsteps coming from behind!

Someone was springing across the hall—and then a pistol barrel prodded into the small of his back!

"That's just what *you're* going to do—drop that gun and turn around." A voice that struggled desperately to be calm barked that in his ear, and the Spider's heart sank. "Drop it, I tell you!"

It was Ed Morgan at his back—with a gun and out to avenge Phil Dunning against all who came his way. There was no time to argue with him, even if he would listen. The Spider's gun dropped to the floor. He would have to chance taking Morgan off guard, to whirl and—

Before the Spider could do that, a new interruption came from the hallway. Feet raced down the stairs, an automatic cracked—and a bullet thudded into the wooden pillar beside his head. That was another thug thudding down the steps—wild-eyed, snarling-faced, gun blazing.

If the petrified group in the living-room had been like statuary a moment before, that shot broke the spell and transposed them suddenly into whirlwind action. Peggy screamed. One of the embalmers leaped head-first through a window. The other flung himself to the floor and scuttled to a rear doorway like a crab. The thug who had recognized the Spider made a dive for the archway, while the Spider whirled and knocked the gun out of Morgan's hand before that surprised young man knew what had happened.

He of the scarred hand took that opportunity to make a break for the doorway, and almost collided with his partner from upstairs as they dashed out. But before the third thug could follow, the Spider had stooped and snatched up Morgan's gun, sending a slug from its barrel through the fellow's brain.

Only Morgan and Peggy had seen that shot. The girl stood against a wall, hands in front of her face to shut out the sight of the corpse. But Morgan was at the Spider's side as he bent over the slain thug and grunted with satisfaction.

"You know him?" Morgan's question was awe-stricken.

"Just a cheap crook," the Spider nodded. He salved his conscience with the thought that all crooks are cheap and worthless. The dead man was Joe Ruigi, one of Duke Samoli's pet hoods.

Samoli was an ambitious gang-leader, ruthless and hungry for power, but too slick and adroit to be enmeshed by the police. A brain and ambition like Samoli's might have conceived this far-reaching scheme for criminal domination. It was like the man to want to set himself up as a dictator. But if it were Samoli who was pulling the strings, it would be suicide for Ed Morgan to attempt his blundering interference. He wouldn't last an hour against such a ruthless crime-boss. Samoli would have him wiped out with as little compunction as he would swat a troublesome fly....

"Let's see what they were up to upstairs," the Spider snapped, and led the way up the steps.

IT TOOK only a glance at the upper floor to reveal that the rooms had been systematically ransacked and looted. Peggy's had been practically torn apart. Every drawer was overturned. Mattress, pillows and chair cushions were slashed open—even dresses torn to pieces.

"They were mighty anxious to find something." The Spider turned to the girl in the doorway. "What was it?"

Ed Morgan opened his mouth as if to protest, but the girl ignored him. Half-turning from them, she lifted her skirt and ran her fingers into the top of her stocking.

"I think it was this," she said tonelessly. "It came yesterday. I tried to get word to Phil, but they wouldn't let me. I was afraid to go to the police. Now it doesn't matter."

The Spider had already unfolded the letter-size sheet of paper. From its white surface a faint typewritten message stared up at him. It was a message printed on an old-style Oliver machine, with a ribbon so old that it barely smudged the paper. But, despite this, its message was cruelly clear—

SLAVES OF THE BLACK MONARCH

Peggy Dunning:

If you value the life of your brother, get in touch with him immediately and warn him that Ownie Garlauf is to be acquitted. If Garlauf is convicted, Dunning will die. Don't make a mistake and take this note to the police—unless you want to die also; you and all the rest of your family. Time is short. Get busy, if you don't want to attend a funeral!

In place of a signature was a crude drawing of a spread-out hand with a red scar slashed across its back. The Spider stared down at that warning—then the distant wail of police sirens rang in his ears. Officers were running across the porch, yelling to be admitted. The Spider made up his mind.

Before Morgan could protest, he thrust the gun that had killed Ruigi into his hand, pressed his fingers firmly around it.

"Hold onto that—it's yours," he gave crisp orders. "When the police want to know what happened, you killed that thug downstairs—understand? You take the credit. I don't want to figure in it at all. I want to be perfectly free to take care of the rest of that gang. The less said about me the better."

Impatiently, a police club smashed through a downstairs window, and heavy-shod feet clumped across the hardwood floors. Before they reached the stairs, the Spider was already out of a back window, racing across a one-story addition at the rear of the building, shimming down a drain-pipe and disappearing in the dark shrubbery, to work his way quietly back to the car.

CHAPTER 3
RENDEZVOUS WITH DEATH

A FEW minutes after the Spider drove away from 85th Road, he stopped his car on a quiet street and went to work. Five minutes later, Richard Wentworth was back at the wheel and the car was speeding back to that sheet-iron garage where it was always kept in readiness. From there, he hailed a taxicab and drove to the Hopecrest Apartments on Central Park West atop which was located his two-story penthouse.

That apartment-house, owned and operated by Wentworth, was his stronghold. Every man employed in it was a tried and trusted retainer, most of them ex-soldiers who had served under Major Wentworth in France during the World War. Even the tenants were hand-picked, and included Police Commissioner Kirkpatrick and the New York County district attorney. More than once Wentworth had found it decidedly advantageous to have such tenants almost at his fingertips.

Stepping into the reception-hall, he came face to face with Martin Egelhart, who was on his way out. Egelhart nodded, but seemed wrapped up in something that was absorbing his entire attention and bringing a sparkle of excitement to his eyes.

What was Egelhart doing in the Hopecrest? Wentworth wondered. From the elevator operator, he learned that the visitor had come down from the tenth floor, on which was located Kirkpatrick's suite. What could have brought him to the police commissioner's apartment at that hour of night? Probably nothing, Wentworth shrugged. But he could not drive from his mind the picture of Egelhart dropping out of the way just in time to avoid that hail of death which cut down his fellows....

Once the elevator deposited him at the top of the shaft, Wentworth walked the stretch of landscaped roof to the penthouse that was a veritable fortress. All the windows in that two-story building were of bulletproof glass, further protected by steel shutters that could be slid into place at a moment's notice. This path across the lawn was the only way in which it could be entered—except by a private elevator within the building itself, known only to Wentworth and his servants.

That elevator ran down to the basement and connected with a tunnel which led to three of a line of garages behind the house. These, in turn, could be opened by means of a moving wall so that egress might be had into the street behind, as well as in front of, the building. Time, money and the results of years of hazardous experience had gone into the construction of that dwelling, and, as he walked along the photo-electric-ray guarded path, Wentworth had the satisfaction of knowing that it was as nearly impregnable as any place can be in this age.

A fitting headquarters for the Spider—though only three people in that whole building knew that its master and the Spider were one. Jackson, Wentworth's chauffeur, who had been a sergeant under the major in France, was one of these. A more obedient and loyal friend and servant no man could have asked. Ram Singh, huge, bearded Sikh descendant of a long line of Hindu warriors, was another; and the ties which bound his proud allegiance to his master were things which he never mentioned—and never forgot.

The third was old Jenkyns, tried and tested butler, who met him solicitously as he stepped up to the door. Jenkyns never seemed to sleep, and, always at his post, anticipated his master's slightest desires.

"No call from Miss van Sloan, Jenkyns?" Wentworth arched his brows. "I expected her to be after me before this. Better get her suite for me—at the Coronet in Atlantic City."

The call came through almost as soon as he reached his private rooms on the floor above. Jenkyns announced that Nita was on the wire.

"I know you're going to say that I intended this all along," Wentworth started diffidently, "but I couldn't get away today. I've been tied up every minute—just got back to the apartment. And that's not all of it. I'm afraid I'll not be able to get away tomorrow." He waited a moment for Nita to show her disappointment. But only silence came over the wire. "I'll be with you the moment I can get things in hand. Meanwhile, I want you to take it easy. Get all the rest you can. Understand?"

Yes, Nita understood. She knew that something unavoidable must have detained him and she would, of course, wait for him. She gossiped idly about the Haley party and blew him a kiss over the phone—but there was something oddly evasive in her manner—even her voice.

WENTWORTH HUNG up the receiver, thoughtfully. Was she hurt? Was that why she had not seemed distressed by his changed plans? Was that why she had not questioned him to find out what was delaying him in New York? It wasn't like Nita to become so disinterested. What explanation could there be?

As he lay back on his bed, mulling over her unexpected behavior, the radio, which he had turned on, switched from a music program to a news flash:

"Stud Rickert, on trial for the murder of Irving Fisher, during a hold-up of Fisher's shoe store, has just been acquitted by a jury in the Bronx County Court," the announcer intoned. "Judge Alvin Davis, who presided, considered the verdict so flagrant a miscarriage of justice that he held the jurors in their box for five minutes while he administered a vitriolic tongue-lashing."

Wentworth knew every detail of this Rickert case. It was cold-blooded vicious murder, unnecessary and inexcusable—and yet the jury had turned Rickert loose! Judge Davis' reaction was perfectly understandable, yet those jurymen were only human. When Wentworth remembered what had happened that afternoon to twelve men who had dared to try to do their duty, he could hardly blame these men for saving their own skins.

But this clearly intimidated verdict in the Bronx was no exception. From all parts of the city the story was the same. Everywhere, justice was being prostrated beneath the deadly rule of an underworld ruthlessly wiping out all opposition. Death was the swift lot of any who dared oppose it. By now, Wentworth realized, the master-mind behind this plan of terror must know that the Spider had seen fit to challenge his ruthless campaign. Thanks to the escape of those thugs from the Dunning house, he had been warned and was undoubtedly already laying plans to deal with the Spider as he had already dealt with those who had the temerity to stand in his way!

Now it was war, death for the loser—and the trump cards secure in the fist of the enemy!

KIRKPATRICK TELEPHONED while Wentworth was reading the newspaper account of the disturbance at the Dunning home the night before. It had been, the paper said, a burglary, and some of Peggy Dunning's jewelry had been taken. There was no mention of the Spider, and the killing of Ruigi was credited to Ed Morgan, who had been taken into protective custody—just as Wentworth hoped would happen. If the terrified embalmers were not too scared to remember the Spider's appearance, they had evidently wisely determined to keep their mouths shut and avoid trouble.

Kirkpatrick now asked him to come down to his office, which was exactly the invitation Wentworth wanted. But the moment he stepped into the commissioner's private office his face filled with concern.

Stanley Kirkpatrick looked ill. Rings were under his eyes and his usually florid face appeared mottled, lined. He looked as if he had not slept for a week, and the eyes which glanced up from the reports spread before him were weary, haggard.

"I want to ask a few more questions about that slaughter in Penn Station, Dick," he greeted. "I've asked thousands of questions already, but the sum of the information gleaned is absolutely nothing. At least one killer was there in a crowded station, operating a machine gun that slaughtered eight people and wounded six others. Yet nobody will admit having seen him! Dozens of people saw him, must have been right beside him— but they don't dare open their mouths!

"I can't blame them—that's the worst of it. Talkers are wiped out too quickly—even when they wear judges' robes. Last night, Judge Davis ripped up a Bronx jury for turning Stud Rickert loose—and at four o'clock this morning his home was invaded and he and his wife shot down in cold blood. There's not a clue to the identity of the murderers. Not a thing but a number of fingerprints on the door—and *they're* utterly baffling.

"They're the same prints we found on the painters' scaffold over in Long Island City. The same that were found on the door of Phil Dunning's home, out in Richmond Hill, after thugs broke in there last night and wrecked the place. But this *can't* all be the work of one man, Dick! We've found those fingerprints in a dozen of places, all over the map. I admit that the thing has me at my wit's end—"

"I see you've locked up that Morgan chap so that they can't wipe him out," Wentworth hazarded.

"That was the idea, of course, when we picked him up," Kirkpatrick nodded. "But even that seems to be going haywire. Ten minutes ago, I heard from District Attorney Cunnison, of Queens, and he tells me his grand jury is getting out of hand. Disregarding his advice, they want to indict Morgan for that killing—which any damned fool knows was self-defense and legitimate protection of the Dunning home. They've received

Suddenly two blazing automatics whipped out in Blinky McQuade's hands— blasting quick death.

their orders and are terrified. So now we'll probably see an innocent man indicted and convicted because he dared to shoot
down an armed robber in his fiancée's home!"

This was a development Wentworth had not anticipated. It

gave him a new appreciation of the devilish ingenuity of the crime master. Not only could he thwart the Law at his pleasure, but he could twist it to his own ends—make a mockery of Justice and compel it to become his private executioner!

Kirkpatrick seemed to read his thoughts.

"The man behind these crimes is the cleverest crook I've ever encountered," he said soberly. "The organization he's building up is a menace that's appalling."

The tired gray eyes studied Wentworth while Kirkpatrick weighed his words carefully.

"I've always had a great respect for the Spider, even though I cannot countenance his methods and am sworn to apprehend him," he said slowly. "I never would have believed that he could stoop to a level as low as this. I don't want to believe it now. But only a man of his imagination and ability could engineer a campaign so audacious and far-reaching. Dick, if I find that the Spider has a hand in this I'll slam him into the electric chair, if it's the last thing I ever do!"

"And I'll help you do it, Kirk." Wentworth held out his hand as he rose to leave. "That's a promise you can call me on, any time."

FROM THE commissioner's office, Richard Wentworth went to a telephone booth and called Mike Fogarty, a trusted private detective whom he employed from time to time. He instructed Fogarty to watch developments in Ed Morgan's case and report anything of importance. Then he headed for that district east of the Bowery that seems to have been laid out with as little attempt at regularity as the haphazard designs in a kaleidoscope.

In one of its most chopped-up and congested sections is a spot where Holian Alley and Pallin Place intersect and form a sharp V. The rear of the second house from the tip of the V on Holian Alley looks out onto a dark little court that also serves as a backyard for the corresponding house on Pallin Place—a circumstance that has often been of great assistance to the dwellers of both tenements in facilitating their hasty coming and goings.

Wentworth turned into the dingy doorway on "Holy Alley," as its denizens dubbed the squalid, filth-littered canyon, and climbed to the second floor, where he let himself into a dank, evil-smelling room, For a moment, he stood beside the window, looking down into the court. There were two loungers squatting on overturned ashcans and apparently arguing meaninglessly. But as he watched them he was fairly certain that their eyes strayed continually to his window. They were there to watch his room.

The room was cheerless and cheaply furnished, on a par with any of the others in the building. But as soon as Wentworth had locked the door and pulled down the shades the seeming tumbledown furniture began to reveal unsuspected potentialities.

By a pressure of the fingers, applied to the center panel at the head of the old wooden bed, the whole thing could be made to open outward, revealing a complete kit of make-up materials and various tools invaluable to the Spider. The antique mattress was no thing of beauty, but, when Wentworth turned up the worn ticking edge at one end, he brought to light a concealed zipper that opened a slit three feet long. This revealed a safe depository for the suit he was wearing—clothing that might prove embarrassing if found in Blinky McQuade's meagerly furnished closet.

When Wentworth was finished with the make-up box, and had supplied himself with an outfit from the closet, it was Blinky McQuade who turned off the gas light and locked the door behind him. The loungers were gone from the court when he crossed it, leaving by way of the Pallin Place building. It was nearly noon, and he had an appointment with Reef Schneider at the Bit House.

SCHNEIDER WAS waiting for him, when he passed through the formalities of entering and stepped into the smoke-foul barroom. But even in that semi-opaque atmosphere he could see at once that the old fellow was terrified. McQuade took him by the arm and elbowed him up to the bar, ordering two glasses of Kentucky Gold. But his favorite beverage did not interest Schneider today. He wetted his lips uncertainly with the end of his tongue. When he lifted the glass his hand trembled so violently that the whisky sloshed out over his fingers.

"What's eatin' yuh, Reef?" Blinky asked for the second time.

The old man's attempt to answer was an inarticulate gurgle that almost choked him as his eyes flitted fearfully toward the end of the bar.

Wonderingly, Blinky glanced in that direction—and only the hooded glasses concealed the amazement that leaped into his eyes! There, not more than six feet away from him, a man was lifting a glass of whisky to his lips with a hand vividly scarred as if a knife had recently laid open the flesh just above the knuckles!

Above this livid scar, dark, poisonous eyes glared at him—and, as the hand went down, he stared into the vicious face of Ownie Garlauf!

Garlauf, there at large in the Bit House... That meant that he was out on bail—that some judge, trembling for his life, had signed the order which opened the prison gates to him... But that scar was identical with that blazed on the hand of the machine-gun killer on the painters' scaffold in Long Island City—when Garlauf had been sitting in the courtroom! It was the same scar that had been on the hand of the thug in the Dunning home last night—*and that thug was not Ownie Garlauf....*

Amazed, baffled as he was, Blinky was not unaware of a stir behind him. Those who stood near were edging away, giving him room, others ranging themselves behind him so that his way to the adjoining room was cut off. When he turned back to where Reef Schneider had been standing the space was empty, and Wentworth caught a glimpse of the old man worming his way frantically across the room.

Schneider had located the man with the scarred hand, all right—and baited a death-trap with him. That trap was to be sprung now.

Blinky McQuade glanced fearfully up and down the bar. Eyes were watching him from every side. With trembling fingers, he lifted his glass and gulped his drink, then backed away from the bar, edging his way toward the door. But the door was locked, and the doorkeeper nowhere to be seen. Those lowering-faced thugs, who had taken positions behind him, were following. They were close at his back, hands thrust into coat pockets that tilted upward suggestively.

With elaborate deliberation Garlauf turned from the bar, and his hand slid down into his own topcoat pocket. His ugly face was twisted into a nasty grin, the devilish light of the born killer gleaming in his eyes.

"Get goin', rat!" He nodded toward an inner hallway that led to rooms Blinky had never penetrated. "Move—or you'll get it here!"

But Balmy was hovering close by, little eyes narrowed and broken-nosed face filled with anxiety. Blinky glanced at the husky ex-pugilist, but saw that no hope could be expected from him. Balmy was interested only in the safety of his place, and wanted no killing in his barroom. What went on down that corridor that led to the rear of the building was none of his business.

Cringing, sniffling, Blinky started down the dimly lit hall-way, every muscle alert for the slightest break. Momentarily, he expected the unloosed fury of those cowardly guns to pour lead into his back. In the open doorway at the end of that hall, he hesitated. The bare room was lit only by one grimy electric bulb; he saw that the door was thick and sheathed with metal. Soundproof! This barren, unfurnished room was the Bit House's execution-chamber. Once that door closed behind his assassins, those murderous guns would sieve his body with hot lead!

SLAVES OF THE BLACK MONARCH

This was his reward for prying—death, quick, inescapable. Even now, as he looked Sudden Death in the face, Blinky McQuade could not help but admire the smooth efficiency with which this new power in the underworld removed the slightest interference.

FOR A moment he cringed on the threshold. Then a gun-muzzle jabbed him in the back. Tremblingly, he staggered into the room, half-turned to face his executioners, appeared to wilt back against the wall as the door clicked shut—but the sound of that latch was blotted out by the thunder of two roaring automatics!

As he half-slumped to the floor, Blinky McQuade's hands grasped at his chest seeming to ward off the bullets that would tear the life out of him—then suddenly those hands both whipped clear, each clutching an automatic blasting quick death. Ownie Garlauf's grinning mouth dropped open—almost disintegrated as a bullet smashed through his upper lip and a round, black hole mushroomed the center of his forehead. One of his confederates clutched at his chest and fell twitching to the floor, with a bullet in his heart. The other managed to fire his gun, sending a bullet into the wall where the supposedly helpless target had been cringing. But before he could squeeze the trigger again scorching lead ripped his gun-hand to pieces and a second bullet tore through his skull.

Fast as those twin automatics had flashed into view, they slipped back to their shoulder holsters. Blinky leaped to the body of Ownie Garlauf, grabbed up his right hand. As he lifted the limp fingers, the coat and shirt sleeves slipped back over the wrist. Then Blinky saw that the hand was actually encased in a skin-fitting glove zippered shut from a point near the base of the palm to three or four inches above the wrist. The glove seemed made of human skin or a remarkable counterpart for it, and was vividly marked with the now familiar scar. A perfect job—even to fingertips fashioned to simulate human skin and leave prints wherever they touched!

From a vest pocket, Blinky brought out a small cigarette lighter. His fingers manipulated the bottom so that it slipped open, then pressed against Ownie Garlauf's forehead. When Blinky withdrew it, the small, blood-red replica of a spider was imprinted on the whitening skin—a spider seemingly crawling toward the round crater from which Garlauf's congealing life-blood was still seeping!

Blinky sprang to the other bodies, running his fingers through the pockets of their clothing. In one coat he was rewarded by finding another of those remarkable gloves. He thrust it into his inside pocket beside the one taken from Garlauf.

Every second was precious now. Swiftly, he hurried to one of the shaded windows, pulled up the blind and banged his elbow through the pane of glass. Unfastening the heavy metal shutters, he threw them open wide—then collapsed in a sniveling heap at the far side of the room.

When the door opened cautiously, and heads poked warily through the aperture, Blinky was still cringing there, wringing his hands as he stared at the dead bodies.

"There—there was a man in here," he babbled. "He started shootin' the minute the door was shut. God, I never saw such shootin'—he cut the whole three of 'em down before they could touch him. I dropped on the floor an' he never even looked at me."

Balmy was first in the room. With only a glance at the twisted corpses, he strode to the smashed window, looked out into the littered back yard.

"That's the way he went out," Blinky mumbled. "The winder was busted in, an' he climbed right through it."

"That's how he got out, all right," Balmy grunted, "but what I wanna know is how in hell he got in." For a moment he glared at Blinky suspiciously. Then he bent over Ownie Garlaufs corpse and his attitude underwent a startling change. "God!" he swore under his breath. "The Spider!"

Awe and respect—almost veneration—was in his tone. When he straightened, he turned belligerently on the curious onlookers who had followed him.

"You're layin' off this guy, y' understand?" he flicked a thumb toward Blinky McQuade. "If you got any arguments with him, you settle 'em outside. The Spider did this—an' if *he's* int'rested enough in this guy to save his neck, I'm not takin' any chances havin' him bumped off here."

But Balmy's protection was hardly needed, for, after his customers had stared down at that crimson spider, new respect was in their hard faces for Blinky McQuade. Nobody made an attempt to stop him when he walked down the hallway. The outer door opened magically for him.

FROM A drugstore booth a few blocks away, Blinky called his apartment. Jackson answered, and his voice filled with relief when he recognized Wentworth's voice.

"I wanted to get in touch with you all morning, sir," he exclaimed agitatedly. "Miss van Sloan was here shortly after you left. She wanted to know where you were. When we couldn't tell her, she said she would wait until you came back, and proceeded to make herself comfortable. About twenty minutes later, another young lady arrived—a Miss Peggy Dunning. She seemed excited and said that you told her to come here if she had anything to tell you. I couldn't get any more information out of her, but, while I was talking to her, Miss van Sloan walked into the library and introduced herself.

"She gave me the sign to leave, and there was nothing I could do but go. When I passed through the room a little later, I caught enough of their conversation to hear Miss Dunning speaking about a man named Sam Baumann—Uncle Sam, she called him. And then there was something about a pawnbroker and jewelry. They left together right after that. I tried to detain them, but Miss van Sloan had suddenly decided that she couldn't wait any longer."

"Very good, Jackson," Wentworth approved absent-mindedly, while his thoughts were wrestling with this new development. "Keep yourself in readiness near the phone. I'll call if I need you."

So Nita was back in town, had contacted Peggy Dunning and taken the girl under her wing... That meant that she was sitting in the game, dealing herself a hand even before she knew what the stakes were... In many another crime-adventure, Nita van Sloan and he had worked both side by side and independently. Often, the assistance she had rendered was invaluable, but now he wished with all his heart that she had stayed down there in Atlantic City where he had sent her....

Suddenly, it dawned upon him why her voice had sounded so odd over the phone. He hadn't talked with Nita at all! The girl on the other end of the wire was a dummy stationed there to impersonate her—which meant that Nita had probably been in the city last night. Her call at the apartment this morning had been deliberately timed not to find him at home—so that she could question Jackson and Jenkyns or try to pry information out of Ram Singh.

Hopefully, he dialed the number of her apartment, but there was no answer or word for him at the desk. He had tried to sidetrack her, and now Nita wanted none of his assistance. At that very moment, she was somewhere in the city, matching wits with a devil more cold-bloodedly ruthless than any the Spider had ever encountered!

The battle on his hands was already terrific. Now, added to his burdens, would be the struggle to reach Nita's side in time—before the Scarred Hand struck her, too, down. He must move fast.

CHAPTER 4
UNCLE SAM

RICHARD WENTWORTH was a splendid actor, but Nita van Sloan had been his appreciative audience too often to be entirely taken in by his performance, and, as he had rushed her down the stairway to her train in the Penn Station,

Before Nita or Peggy could move, their arms were twisted up behind them.

she was anything but satisfied. It was not like Dick to be half an hour late. She could see that he was on tenterhooks to get away at the earliest possible moment.

But at least she could thwart that. As the train left the platform, she smiled enigmatically. The more she thought about it, the more thoroughly she was convinced that she was being deliberately shipped to Atlantic City to get rid of her.

"The Spider again," she whispered.

Nita could hardly be blamed if the mental vision of the black-hatted and caped Spider stirred a mixture of strange emotions within her. She was Richard Wentworth's fiancée. Dick loved her; of that she had no doubt. She would have been Mrs. Richard Wentworth years back if only his heart dictated the course of their lives—if the Spider had not stood in the way.

So, in a way, she feared and hated the grim figure of justice which dominated Wentworth's life. But she was also fiercely proud of the man she loved....

She knew that there would be no real happiness for Richard Wentworth if ever he abandoned his crusade. So long as the Spider beckoned him, so long as his blood leaped and pounded to the thrill of fighting the cunning brains of those who crucified Society, there was no peace for him in enforced retirement.

And, because she loved him so understandingly, this girl, who could have selected a husband from the highest walks of life, chose to wait—to share the perils and hardships of his chosen calling with her man. If she could not be his wife, at least she could be his comrade.

She knew that her fears were verified the next morning when

57

she picked up the New York newspapers and read the account of the Penn Station massacre. Instead of planning to join her at the seaside resort for a well earned vacation, he had artfully arranged to get her out of the way so that he could plunge into another game of life and death—one so dangerous that he did not even want her to be in the city while it was being waged....

That was why he had been so insistent on the four o'clock train. He wanted to be right there in the station when that bloody slaughter began. Yes, and that probably accounted for the strange lack of preparation she had noticed at the Haleys' party last night; they hardly seemed to know what the whole thing was about. Undoubtedly, it was because Dick Wentworth had pulled that party out of his hat and dumped it, full-blown, in their surprised laps!

As she patched the pieces together, her worry for Dick's safety grew, and a dangerous sparkle glinted in her dark eyes. To reconcile herself to his precarious occupation, while she knew what he was doing and could help him, was one thing. But to be shielded while he faced unknown perils....

Immediately, she set to work making her plans, and by noon she had located a girl whose voice sounded sufficiently like her own to do over the telephone. With half an hour's coaching, the girl knew just what to say and how to parry questions when Wentworth called.

BY LATE afternoon, Nita was back in New York. The evening papers were ablaze with headlines on the Garlauf jury slaughter and quick to tie it up with the killing of George Roeble the day before. This, she was sure, was the case occupying Dick, but, try as she would, she could get no direct line on it. Nor could she locate him. By having friends telephone him, she ascertained that he was not in his apartment and that his man did not know when he would return. A search of his usual haunts was equally unproductive, and, by midnight, she had still found no trace of him.

Jackson, Jenkyns and Ram Singh, she knew, were three of the most tight-lipped individuals God had ever made, but the next morning she decided to see what information she could get from them. From a cab at the curb across the way, she waited until Wentworth left the building, and, shortly afterward, went up to his apartment.

As she expected, her questioning obtained nothing.

"This is the master's evil day that he should have missed the *memsahib,*" Ram Singh assured her with a low bow—but, beyond that, entirely uncommunicative.

"Mr. Wentworth came home quite late last evening," old Jenkyns admitted. "He said nothing beyond instructing me to telephone your hotel. He did not say where he was going this morning."

Only Jackson rewarded her visit in the slightest degree. He was surprised to see her; uneasy, worried. All too plainly, he would have liked nothing better than to report her arrival to Dick, and it seemed to add nothing to his composure when she strolled up to the second floor and made herself at home in Wentworth's living-room.

Nita was beginning to berate herself for having let Dick get away that morning. She was undecided whether to wait here for his return or make another effort to locate him. Then she caught the sound of a strange voice in the library—a woman.

Carefully, she opened the door, and looked out at a very pretty young blonde who seemed in a great state of agitation. She wanted to see Mr. Wentworth. Nobody but Mr. Wentworth would do. Mr. Wentworth had told her to come here when she had any information to give him. She was mauling her handbag in such nervous fingers that it seemed on the point of disintegrating. Then Nita saw that her concern was more than uneasiness—stark terror.

Jackson was getting nowhere with her, and Nita decided it was time to interfere.

"How do you do?" she smiled, stepping through the doorway. "I am a close friend of Mr. Wentworth's. Perhaps I can help you."

Jackson, she saw from the corner of her eyes, had almost fallen off his chair. She heard his gulp back whatever had come to the tip of his tongue. She turned, smiling.

"Perhaps you had better mix a cocktail for us, Jackson," she suggested. "A Bacardi, Miss Dunning? Jackson mixes them perfectly."

Eagerly, Peggy Dunning grasped at the opportunity to talk to another woman. Almost before Jackson was out of the room she began.

"I don't know whether I should bother you with this, Miss van Sloan, but Mr. Wentworth told me to come. That was last night when he came to see me. I didn't think then that there would be anything to tell him, but this morning—"

"Yes," Nita interrupted softly, "just take it easy and tell me about it slowly and quietly—there's no need to be excited."

"Well," the girl pitched her voice lower, "you know how my brother was killed yesterday—and you probably read about how we were held up and robbed last night.  About eight-thirty this morning, I received a phone call from a man who said his name was Sam Baumann—Uncle Sam, he called himself. He has a pawnshop at this address on the Bowery." She took a slip of paper out of her bag. "He said that he has something he thinks belongs to me—something that was brought to him last night. He was very mysterious about it, but I think it must be some of my jewelry taken in the robbery.

"He said that if I came to his store today I could have it. At first, I was going to go to the police. But I don't dare now. Not after what happened to my brother. Last night, when we were held up, my fiancé, Ed Morgan, killed one of the thieves. The police have him in jail now—as a material witness, they say. But I'm so worried. There is nobody else I can turn to, so I thought of Mr. Wentworth's offer—I thought he would be able to tell me what to do. Perhaps, I'd better forget about the jewelry, altogether. But this Uncle Sam seemed quite anxious to have me come and get it—"

At once Nita sensed that there was more to this apparently innocent call from the pawnbroker than appeared on the surface. Perhaps it was just the lead she had been seeking!

"I don't think we had better wait until Mr. Wentworth

returns," she told Peggy Dunning. "Time may be precious, so I'm going with you myself." And despite Jackson's almost pathetic attempts to delay them, she carried the girl off.

NOT UNTIL they were seated in a taxi-cab, bound downtown to the quiet Claremore Hotel, did she reveal the rest of the plan rapidly formulating in her mind. Then she spoke more freely.

"That telephone call sounds to me decidedly like a lead-on—like bait," she said soberly. "Yet it isn't the sort of thing that can be handled by simply ignoring it. I'm afraid you're in trouble, Peggy—I'm going to call you that, and I wish you'd call me Nita.

"The Claremore, where this cab is taking us, is a nice, quiet hotel where nobody will bother you—and where nobody is likely to think of looking for you. I want you to register there and stay for a few days until we find out just what this is all about. Not under your own name—suppose you sign up as 'June Madison?' I'll go in with you now, and I'll keep in touch with you constantly."

Peggy Dunning was trembling, but she took hold of herself when she signed her new alias on the hotel register and told the clerk her bag would arrive later in the day. In her room, Nita faced her and went over her story from the beginning—went over every detail, in which there was no mention of the surprising visit of the Spider—and, as she listened, Nita realized that the girl was undoubtedly in serious danger. Danger, she suspected, which arose from her possession of that threatening note.

"And that note," she asked for the second time, "isn't there any way you can get hold of it?"

Peggy Dunning was uncomfortable. A hint of color rose in her pale cheeks, but again her answer was vague. She had given it to a friend for safe-keeping—a will-o'-the-wisp, John Willetts.

"And you don't know where to locate him?" Nita prodded.

"No, he just comes to our house sometimes," lamely.

The girl was keeping something back, that was apparent. But Nita could see nothing to be gained by making an issue of it. Something far more important might be accomplished by visiting this Uncle Sam and finding out why he was so anxious to return stolen jewelry....

SAM BAUMANN'S pawnshop was located on the ground floor of a corner building. It was an ancient, ramshackle structure that looked as if it had leaned against the elevated structure for support for many years and, now that the old pillars were gone, was ready to topple over into the street. The dusty and discolored windows were piled high with an accumulation of junk.

Going through the old doorway was like stepping back into the musty past, and the inside of the shop was packed even more closely with trinkets and gadgets that had been fashionable in by-gone generations. Behind the worn counter, in the midst of the reliquary, stood a thin, wiry old man with sparse gray hair and old-fashioned, silver-rimmed spectacles.

His face was soft and benign, but his gray eyes, when he peered over the top of his glasses, were keen, alert. He smiled benevolently as Nita and Peggy Dunning approached his counter. But when Peggy introduced herself his smile vanished and his face became secretive while he hunched over between his showcase as if to get as close to them as possible. Uneasily, his eyes darted around the store, seemingly fearful of eavesdroppers.

"Ah, yes. You came to see what I have for you," he nodded. "And this young lady—she is a friend of yours? Yes, yes, I see. Now, if you will just wait a moment—" He disappeared through a curtained doorway at the end of the counter.

At first, there were the sounds of his moving about in the rear room. Then silence stretched on into minutes before he came brushing back through the faded curtains.

"You must excuse the delay," he apologized, "but it isn't safe to keep—ah—items of this nature out here in the shop."

Out of his pocket he drew a dainty wrist-watch set in a diamond and sapphire bracelet.

"That's mine!" Peggy exclaimed. "Ed gave it to me for my birthday last year. You can see my initials on the back of the case. It was stolen last night—"

"Ah, that's what I feared," Uncle Sam shook his head regretfully. "I suspected as much when I read the newspaper this morning. In this business, one can't be too careful. There was something queer—something mysterious—about the man who brought it to me—"

"Do you know where you can locate him?" Nita interposed.

For a moment, the old eyes studied her carefully, as if Baumann had just become aware of her presence. Then he nodded.

"Yes, I think I can locate him. But, of course, I can't tell you where to find him. Any—ah—negotiations will have to be conducted through me. This watch was offered to me for sale, conditionally; only if you did not want it, Miss Dunning. I can recover the rest of your jewelry for you, also—if you are willing to return a note which the man who holds it seems to want. He said that you would know what note he means. If you will surrender it to me, he will exchange the jewelry for it."

"But how do we know that we will receive the jewelry once we give up the note?" Nita intervened before Peggy had a chance to reveal that she no longer had it in her possession. "Before we could consider surrendering it, we'd have to see all the missing pieces."

Again the old head shook sorrowfully.

"You do not trust me," he reproached, "and I can't blame you. I am only a third party in this transaction, handling a matter very distasteful to me. It is only because I thought that I could help you to recover your valuables—"

Suddenly, the door was thrown open, and three men surged into the stuffy shop—grim-faced, with hands in coat pockets. Uncle Sam's eyes widened, his face went a shade whiter. He tried to step behind one of his cases. It was too late.

"No, you don't, grampa!" one of the trio barked, and an automatic trained on Baumann's stomach.

Before Nita or Peggy could move, their right arms were grabbed, twisted up behind their backs and they were forced toward the rear of the store.

"One peep out o' you, girlie, an' you get a clout over the head," the fellow who had hold of Nita warned. She attempted no resistance as he herded her behind the counter and through the curtained doorway.

ONLY TWO of the men came through that doorway, the other evidently remaining outside to keep Baumann cowed. The back room into which the girls were dragged was evidently the old man's living quarters. A couch stood against one wall, and the place also contained a wardrobe, bureau, table with piled-up dishes and cutlery, and a few chairs. Brutally, Nita's captor threw her down on the couch, wrenching her arm almost out of its socket.

"You're the Dunning dame, ain'cha?" he turned to Peggy. When she nodded in mute acknowledgment, he reached out and took her pocketbook, turned it inside out over the table and ransacked it.

With a grunt of disgust, he turned back.

"All right, sister," he growled, "if you want it this way you can have it," and he took hold of the top of her dress and started to unfasten it.

Peggy pleaded with them and swore that they would find nothing they sought concealed on her. Tears were running down her cheeks. Callously, they stripped her of every garment, until she stood, cowering, without a stitch to cover her.

Beyond a smirk of appreciation, they paid scant attention to her nakedness. Her clothing alone interested them, as they fingered each garment, held it up to the light, searching for the note they were sure she must have on her. So absorbed were they that they did not notice Nita. She had slipped off the couch, worked her way noiselessly toward the table, hardly moving until she was close enough to leap to it and seize the carving knife she had seen among the cutlery.

The point of that knife was pricking the back of his neck before one of the startled thugs knew what was happening. Nita's fingers closed over the barrel of his automatic, wrenching it from his hand.

"Don't move!" she warned. Then, to his partner, when the pistol was safely in her hand, "Drop your gun on the floor— unless you want it shot out of your hand!"

The second automatic thudded to the carpeted floor. Nita stepped out from behind her human shield to scoop it up, while the thugs cursed her vilely. Their eyes were venomous, as she covered them and forced them back to the wall. They did not dare try to make a break in the face of those steady muzzles, yet the guns could not gag them.

"Smart girl, ain'tcha?" one of them snarled. "But what the hell good's this gonna do yuh?" He turned his tongue on Peggy. "*You* oughta know enough to do what you're told by this time. Looks like you need another lesson. Maybe you want that boyfriend o' yours to get the same dose they handed your brother—"

Peggy Dunning's eyes widened with terror.

"Pull anything fast, an' you're signin' that guy's death warrant," the other added. "He can be reached in a cell even quicker than in a courtroom, an' if you don't believe it—"

"No—no!" Peggy screamed hysterically. "Oh, God, you *can't* hurt him! You can't—"

Sobbing wildly, she suddenly threw herself across the room. Without warning, she flung both arms around Nita, held her tight. Instantly, the thugs pounced upon Nita, wresting their weapons from her fingers. Brutally, one of them lashed out with his fist—and Nita spun across the room, to slump at the side of the couch in a heap, stunned.

Sick with horror, she watched while they grabbed Peggy.

"Where's that note?" they snarled. "Spit it out!"

But the girl grimly kept her lips clenched.

Savagely, they twisted a slender arm behind her back until her head was bent almost to the floor. Beads of perspiration stood out on Peggy's forehead, but her eyes were grimly defiant. Then one man lit a cigarette, puffed on it until the coal glowed red— and pressed it against the tender skin low on her neck. A scream of sheer agony burst from her as she writhed away.

"The Spider!" she gasped. "The Spider has it!"

"So-o-o," the cigarette-wielder purred, "the Spider has it. And where is the Spider?"

"I don't know!" she shrieked. "I swear to God I don't know! I never saw him before last night. He took the note and disappeared!—"

The coal seared into the girl's flesh again—and Nita could stand no more. Somehow, she catapulted herself up from the floor and leaped at the torturer. Her teeth closed on his gun-wrist, and the automatic dropped to the floor as he yelped with pain. In an instant, she had it. She fired at the fellow holding Peggy. With a howl of terror, he released the girl, bolted for the curtained doorway, barely dashing through ahead of his confederate.

WARILY, NITA stood on guard with the captured gun

while Peggy got into her clothes. She cautiously parted the curtains and peered out into the shop. But there was no sign of the hold-up men. Old Uncle Sam was staggering up from the floor, clasping his head as he half-fell over the counter.

There was no time to see how seriously he had been hurt. Those thugs might be back at any moment with reinforcements, and Nita had no desire for another meeting. The Bowery was almost empty as she stepped out onto the street. Nobody paid the two girls any attention when they hailed a cab and directed the driver to the Claremore Hotel.

Nita leaned back against the leather cushion, reviewing the startling happenings of the past half-hour. So the Spider had taken a hand in the Dunning case; he had been in the set-to in Richmond Hill and now had in his possession the note which these criminals would go to any limit to recover.

Gradually, she drew out Peggy Dunning's story. Before they had reached the hotel, she determined to know more about that attack on Uncle Sam Baumann's place. She wanted another talk with the old man, and that as soon as she could get back to her apartment and lay her hands on something worth pawning.

But her telephone was clamoring when she got back to her own place. It was Commissioner Kirkpatrick.

"Thank God, I got hold of somebody at last," he growled. "Been ringing you all afternoon with no more luck than I've had with Wentworth. I want to talk to you, Nita—right away. Come down here and see me."

"I'm on my way," she replied. As she taxied downtown, a hundred questions and surmises were racing through her mind.

Kirkpatrick did not leave her long in doubt. As soon as he had ushered her to a seat beside his desk, he started long and thoughtfully, apparently endeavoring to read the thoughts behind her smooth forehead.

"Where is Dick?" he asked levelly.

When she shook her head and shrugged, he sighed. Then he sat bolt upright in his chair and leaned toward her, face grave.

"This isn't any of the usual hide-and-seek," he barked. "This is dead serious, Nita. I'm looking for the Spider—and I'm looking for Richard Wentworth. There's no use beating around the bush with you. You know what I think—what I suspect. For a long while, I've been reasonably sure that Richard Wentworth and the Spider were one and the same person. Reasonably sure, but not positive. I've been willing to let it go in recognition of various services the Spider has done for society as a whole.

"But now he has gone too far. Three bodies were found lying in a lot of junk behind a garage, early this afternoon. One was Ownie Garlauf—and the Spider's mark was stamped on his forehead. The evening papers have the story"—he motioned to a pile of black-headlined extras—"and they're howling to high Heaven, adding these three murders to the list of unpunished killings they print on the front page every day."

"But, Commissioner—" Nita started to protest.

"How does this concern Wentworth?" he cut her short. "Here's how. I know that he's been steamed up about this wave of lawlessness, just as I have. I've had a pretty shrewd hunch that he was playing a hand in the game. Now, I'm sure of it. He's taking the law into his own hands because we're falling down. But he's only making matters worse.

"I'm delighted to know that Garlauf got what was coming to him; I admit that. But, by God, I'm going to round up the Spider and send him to the chair for that murder—*no matter who he is!* I've been trying to get hold of Dick all afternoon. If he's not guilty, I want him to give himself up. If he doesn't, I'm going to get him. That's final, Nita. Now, get the word to him."

Often Nita had wondered how long Kirkpatrick could be held in check. How long would it be before he blew up and called a spade a spade? Now, that time had come. The Spider was a hunted creature with a reward hanging over his head, and now Richard Wentworth would become the same fugitive. Unless he gave himself up, the alarm would go out to bring him in, dead or alive—and she did not know where to find him, even if taking him such a message had been of any use!

CHAPTER 5
A DEBT IS PAID

WHEN BLINKY McQuade stepped out of the drug-store telephone booth, after his unsuccessful attempt to reach Nita van Sloan at her apartment, he walked to the file of directories and thumbed through the Manhattan book until he found *Baumann, Samuel, pawnbroker* with an address on the Bowery. This was his quarry, and, fifteen minutes later, he was perched on a stool in a lunch-counter on the corner opposite the pawnshop, nursing cups of poisonous coffee while he kept track of Uncle Sam's patrons.

It took no more than half an hour of such surveillance to

A bleak-faced figure arose among the colored musicians; orange-red flame belched in the banquet-room.

convince him that the broker was a fence—and to concoct a plan which he immediately started putting into execution.

From the Bowery, he made his way toward the river until he reached the little sheet-iron garage where his car was parked—to drive out, a few minutes later, as Richard Wentworth at his smartest. A Richard Wentworth who was received with smiling deference when he walked into a Fifth Avenue jewelry store and asked to see a selection of matched-pearl necklaces. A five-thousand-dollar string suited his fancy, and, with it tucked away in his topcoat pocket, he drove downtown to the Empire State Building, to drop in at an office whose glass door bore the legend—*James Hollingshurst, Investments.*

Wentworth grinned, as he saw the smile of anticipation which welcomed him. Some months before, he had had occasion to use young Hollingshurst in helping to get evidence against a pair of fraudulent promoters. Since then, Jim had been living in hopeful expectancy of the day when he would have another thrilling taste of crime-fighting.

His eyes popped wide when Wentworth opened the pearl-case and slid it across his huge, glass-topped desk.

"That's right—take a good look," Wentworth laughed. "They're yours, you know, and I want you to be able to give the police a good description of them when you get home and find that they've been stolen from your wall-safe."

"Stolen—out of my safe!" Hollingshurst gulped.

"You're getting it down perfect," Wentworth chuckled. "When you reach your apartment tonight, all I want you to do is call the police and report that you found your safe standing open and the pearls missing. They're valued at five thousand dollars— matched pearls—and you're very anxious to recover them. You can add any embroidery you want to the story, as long as you holler loud enough to get a mention in the morning papers."

"But the insurance?" the would-be detective reminded uneasily. "I won't get in a jam with the insurance people, will I? They're tough—"

"No insurance on them," Wentworth reassured him. "No

complications you need worry about—but you'll be helping me a lot if you put this over, Jim. It's important to me that this robbery gets some publicity."

When he left that office and drove the car back to his hide-out garage, he knew that he need have no worry about Hollingshurst. Young Jim would have half the reporters in New York by the ear before he was finished....

The second part of his scheme depended upon being able to locate Reef Schneider, and upon Schneider's willingness to help. SCHNEIDER WASN'T in the Bit House when Blinky McQuade went looking for him there. But, by virtue of the new importance the Spider's activity on his behalf had shed upon him, Blinky was able to wheedle the old man's address from the bartender. It was Holy Alley, just down the street from his own place—a dingy tenement even more dilapidated and noisome than his own.

Reef opened the door on a discreet crack, and, when he recognized his bespectacled visitor, seemed about to slam it shut again. But he thought better, backing away abjectly.

"I didn't mean you no harm, Blinky," he mumbled fearfully. "I just asked around like you told me. I asked about this guy with a scar on the back of his hand—then they come down on me like a ton o' brick. One feller grabbed me an' took me to Ownie Garlauf, an' he made me tell why I wanted to know. He half-choked the life out o' me, so I hadda tell him 'bout you. They said they'd fill me full o' lead, if you was tipped off. What could I do, Blinky?"

"Forget it," he waved aside the old man's anxious explanations.

"Those things happen. That ain't what I come to see you about." He spread out on the greasy-topped table a string of pearls that bugged out Schneider's eyes. "Beauties, ain't they? They're hot, Reef. I gotta unload in a hurry but I wanna decent price. You know this old Uncle Sam Baumann, over on the Bowery? I hear he treats a guy right—"

"Sure, I know him—known him for years." Schneider, the moment he recovered from his amazement, was anxious to placate. "He's the feller for beauties like them. Handles big stuff, he does. We c'n go over there now, if you wanna."

Together, they walked to the Bowery, where Reef Schneider duly introduced and vouched for his friend Blinky McQuade—and then left with the price of four Kentucky Golds clutched in his fist.

Sam Baumann's eyes didn't bug out when he saw the pearls dropped into his hand. But they did sparkle with appreciation, and he fondled the gems lovingly. Then those eyes turned to Blinky, studied him sadly as he shook his head, making low, deprecating sounds behind his teeth.

"Beautiful," he admitted. "But where did you get them—that's the question."

"What's that got to do with it?" Blinky snarled. "I heard you was right—"

"Right—right," old Baumann picked up the word while he shook his head dolefully. His benign face became almost harsh with rebuke. "It is never right to steal—and these pearls are stolen. Dangerous business," he worried. "Sooner or later, there is a slip, and then you are caught. How do I know the police are not looking for this necklace? How do I know they won't come in here any minute to search my place?"

"*You* know they won't," Blinky grinned knowingly. He could not help admiring the engaging old hypocrite. "What'll you give me?"

"Not today!" Uncle Sam protested quickly. "I can't appraise them right away—that takes time. I must have at least until the morning before I can make an offer. You leave them here in my safe, and tomorrow when you come back I'll tell you what they're worth to me."

And by that time, Blinky knew, the sanctimonious old codger would have had a chance to run through the morning papers. Once sure that the gems were really stolen, he would cut his offer in half.

"What name?" Uncle Sam had already slipped the necklace into an envelope, and held his pencil ready.

"McQuade—John A. McQuade," Blinky grumbled.

"Address?"

"Skip that," with a sneer. "I ain't gonna get lost. I'll be seein' you in the morning—an' I know what them babies are worth. Don't forget that."

Blinky's spectacled eyes were alert every moment he was in that shop, but he could detect nothing suspicious. An ordinary fourth-rate hockshop, it might have passed for a curio-shop but for the three balls hanging over the door and the pawn tickets attached to the cheap jewelry in the showcase. Nowhere was there anything that he could remotely connect with Nita or Peggy Dunning, and he wondered whether they had been here yet.

To ask about them was out of the question. The only way to secure any information from old Baumann was to win his confidence—and sell those pearls for a tenth their value. That would take time. For the present, the pawnshop was a dead lead. But there still remained Duke Samoli, and an unsettled account the Spider had opened with his gunmen....

DUKE SAMOLI, too, had seen the wisdom of owning his own home, but the six-story apartment house on West 25th Street, in which he had headquarters, was quite a contrast to the Hope-crest Apartments. From the moment he stepped into the garishly elegant reception-hall, Richard Wentworth felt that he was walking into a trap. The grilled-iron doors closed too solidly behind him, and, he suspected, could be locked securely at the touch of a button. The sleek-haired, olive-skinned doorman sprang up from his desk too alertly, interposed himself too smoothly. It was as if he had rehearsed his part to perfection.

"I'm sorry," he smiled oilily, "but Mr. Samoli isn't in. Perhaps, if you leave your name, he will arrange an appointment."

Wentworth sized him up carefully, running a practiced eye over his expertly tailored uniform. He detected the slight bulge beneath the man's armpits.

"Perhaps he isn't in to most callers, but I want to see him," he said firmly, and started toward the elevator.

"But I tell you he's not in." The dark eyes clouded threateningly, as the fellow backed toward his desk.

"And maybe I'd believe you if I hadn't been across the street and seen him come in five minutes ago," Wentworth snapped.

Before the last word was out of his mouth, he flung himself across the narrow hallway. He grabbed the doorman by the shoulder just as one slim hand darted inside the fellow's coat and the other speared out at a button attached to his desk.

"No, you don't—I'll announce myself," Wentworth clipped, as the doorman went sailing across the hall and crashed into a potted palm.

At the same instant, he dropped to his hands and knees—and the elevator man, who came charging at his back, howled with fright as he went head over heels and landed on his neck against the door.

"Nice teamwork," Wentworth grinned, as his automatic covered the two discomfited employees. "It would be a shame to separate you, so suppose you both get into that elevator and take me up to Samoli's floor. And remember"—one of the automatics prodded the elevator operator's ribs as he sullenly stepped into the cage—"it would be very unfortunate if this car should get out of order."

They stopped at the top floor, and Wentworth shepherded his captives before him, making them lead the way to Samoli's apartment.

"Ring the bell—the right ring," he ordered the doorman. "If you try any signaling you get this gun over your skull—and sometimes a broken head is fatal."

There was nothing treacherous about that ring. Duke Samoli answered it himself, and, the moment he sized up the situation, he burst into embarrassed apologies. But not, however, before Wentworth had caught the glint of fear in the uneasy eyes.

"There was a mistake," Samoli explained hastily. "My man should have known. Come in, Mr. Wentworth—come in."

Wentworth stepped inside cautiously, but Samoli seemed to be alone in the apartment. It took only a glance to see that the big fellow was worried. His eyes were wary, constantly on the alert.

"I want to talk to you about Joe Ruigi," Wentworth came straight to the point "Miss Dunning is a friend of mine, and I want to know what Ruigi was doing out there in her house the other night."

At the mention of the dead thug, Samoli's dark eyes smoldered and a torrent of blistering Sicilian curses spouted from his lips.

"I don't know anything about that," he disclaimed vigorously. "That Ruigi—it's more than three weeks since I saw him."

"I thought you and he used to be pretty thick," Wentworth ventured. "Sort of your right-hand man, wasn't he?"

"One time—yes," the big man admitted, and the lines of worry deepened in his fat face. "That doesn't mean anything now. Same way with most of my best men," he confessed. "They're drifting away—can't count on them anymore."

He read the gleam of understanding in Wentworth's eyes, and his face flushed.

"Maybe I *am* slipping," he glowered, "but I'm not the only one. It's the same way with Dolan, Narocici, Messing—all the big fellers. Somebody's cutting in on us, taking the boys away. If I could get my hands on the rat—"

SAMOLI'S BIG fists were clenching, shaking as if already gripping the throat of his enemy, but he could not camouflage the fear deep in his eyes. His prestige was waning and he was helpless to do anything. That knowledge had unnerved him.

Samoli was another good lead gone sour, but as Wentworth mentally reviewed the events of the past few days he suddenly decided to play a hunch.

"Red Corbin is another chap I want to have a talk with," he switched the conversation. "Don't happen to know where I can locate him tonight, do you, Samoli?"

"Corbin?" The racketeer's eyebrows lifted at mention of the feature writer whose crime reporting had become a sensation. "Sure, I know where he is. There's a big stag party at my place, the Wee Hours, tonight—lot of fellers are throwing it for Arthur Scarborough, the chairman of the swanky grand jury, and took most of the club for a dinner and celebration. Corbin was around this afternoon hitting me up for a press reservation."

Wentworth frowned. Red Corbin wanted to attend that party in the Wee Hours—and Red Corbin had been conveniently on hand at the Penn Station, and again in the Long Island City courtroom, when hell broke loose. In fact, it almost seemed that the man must have second-sight. That was the only way to account for his uncanny knack of being Johnny-on-the-spot whenever a new outrage was staged....

As those thoughts flashed through Richard Wentworth's mind, he recalled the headlines on the late papers. That afternoon, the blue-ribbon New York County grand jury had brought in a first-degree murder indictment against Hymie Glickman, an ex-convict who killed a policeman while holding up a theater box-office. Perhaps, that was just coincidence—but Wentworth scented trouble.

"We're going to the Wee Hours, Samoli," he decided swiftly. "Unless I miss my bet, you'll want to be on hand up there before the night is over. Phone ahead and have them reserve us a table where we'll be able to get a good view of things without being too conspicuous."

THE BANQUET table in the Wee Hours Club was arranged in a huge horseshoe which enclosed two-thirds of the dance-floor and faced the raised orchestra platform at its other end. The table prepared for Wentworth and Samoli was in the second row from the floor and a short distance beyond one end of the horseshoe—a position affording an excellent view of the diners as well as the orchestra and every other part of the house.

Red Corbin, Wentworth soon discovered, was seated with a young girl at a table in approximately the same position at the other side of the floor. He seemed to be giving her undivided attention, and yet Wentworth noticed that, from time to time, his eyes darted expectantly toward the horseshoe table—as if he were waiting for some sort of signal.

It was nearly ten o'clock and most of the diners had completed their meal, when the main lights were dimmed and floodlights turned on the dance-floor. Their radiance reflected from a double-row of white shirtfronts as the men, sitting with their backs to the floor, turned their chairs to enjoy the floor-show.

Alertly, Wentworth watched as soon as his eyes became accustomed to the semi-darkness outside of the lighted space. Everything seemed to be going on as usual. Samoli sat beside him for ten minutes, until one of his waiters called him out to the office. Act after act ran through its routine, and Wentworth could detect nothing out of the ordinary—until a harem-ballet number approached its climax.

The feature dancer discarded veil after veil, working her way down the floor, until she pirouetted in the nude at the top of the horseshoe, directly in front of the guest of honor. Scarborough applauded vigorously, and she plucked a gardenia from her hair, whirled closer to the table and dangled it tantalizingly just out of his reach.

Laughing merrily, he rose to snatch it....

Wentworth was almost caught napping. His eyes, like those of the other watchers, were following the dancer—when, suddenly, he realized that that was exactly what he was expected to do. Instantly, he pivoted his head—and the look on Red Corbin's face told him that the moment had arrived!

Corbin's mouth was pressed into a thin, straight line. His slightly slitted eyes stared out of his white face. His whole body leaned forward, tensed—like a man waiting for a giant firecracker to explode.

Too late Wentworth caught the off-key, saw the colored musicians duck to one side as a black-faced figure rose behind them—and an orange-red flare belched in the darkness.

The laughter froze on Arthur Scarborough's face, his hand clutching his shirtfront just above his heart. It seemed to dissolve into amazement as he felt his life-blood gushing out between his fingers. But, before his body toppled forward and sprawled over the ill-omened horseshoe, his murderer teetered for a split-second and crashed down among the terrified musicians—with one of Wentworth's bullets through the center of his forehead.

Too late Wentworth noticed shadowy, black-faced figures at both doorways from which the performers had filed; too late he noticed others in the passageways leading to the restrooms. Their guns were barking, girls screaming wildly as they threw themselves flat on the dance-floor, men shouting—white-shirted figures slumping out of their chairs or pitching forward over the white-clothed table like clay figures in a shooting gallery!

Outlined pitilessly by the glaring light, they were marks that those devilish sharpshooters could not miss.

DESPERATELY, WENTWORTH triggered his automatic. But he had nothing but the flashes of their guns to locate the killers. The bottle of soda on his table dissolved into a thousand pieces, and he darted behind the protection of a pillar just as bullets smashed into his chair and sent it over backward. To add to the horror of that screaming, thundering bedlam, the lights snapped off, and the place was in darkness.

Now the murderous guns were silent. The killers were making their get-away. But Wentworth was already sprinting across the dance-floor, to fasten his fingers firmly in Red Corbin's collar, just as the fellow tried to get up from his table.

Corbin fought frantically, endeavoring to wriggle out of his coat in a desperate anxiety to escape. But Wentworth's fist smashed into his face and pummeled him into subjection—just as the main lights flashed on and revealed a scene of incredible horror. Everywhere, men were cowering behind pillars or overturned tables, crawling on all fours to where they thought there might be a door and escape.

All but Arthur Scarborough and five of his dinner companions who were still slumped over the remains of their last meal, and a young dancer who lay sprawled in the center of the floor, a hole in the back of her skull.

Wentworth had time only for a glance at that shambles, and then he was dragging Red Corbin into a side room that opened off the main one—a room with heavily curtained windows. Grimly, Wentworth thrust the fellow head-first through the doorway and closed it behind them—to meet his frantic rush with a right to the jaw that dropped him to his knees. Next instant, Wentworth's fingers were fastened in his throat, pushing him relentlessly backward until they were up against the opposite wall.

"You knew this was going to happen here tonight," he gritted. "How? I'm listening. I want to hear plenty of talk, or, by God, you'll not live to say another word!"

"I'll talk!" Corbin gasped. "My neck—give me air! I'll tell you. I couldn't help myself. I had to come—had to be here so that I could write it up. That's all I am—I swear it—just publicity man. Publicity—that's what they want. That's why Egel—"

His voice rose to a scream, slobbered off into a gurgling moan, as a keen-bladed, heavy-handled knife flashed through the air and plunged into his throat, to quiver there just above Wentworth's fingers!

Wentworth whirled, barely in time to catch a glimpse of a scar-marked hand in one of the curtained windows. Then it was gone, and, when he sprang across the room and flung aside the heavy drape, the alley below the open window was empty and quiet. The killer had vanished.

Wentworth stalked out into the main room to hunt up Samoli. He located the proprietor locked in his private office, hammering on the door and clamoring to be freed. When Wentworth turned the key, the big man almost fell through the doorway. His face was green with terror and he appeared on the verge of apoplexy. Unbelievingly, his dilated eyes stared down at the back of his right hand where blood spurted from a nasty cut that had slashed it from side to side!

Queer, animal-like sounds came from his trembling lips, but, when Wentworth tried to question him, he backed away in utter terror. His lips were effectually sealed.

As Wentworth went back to the room where he had left Corbin's body, he saw that his bullets had accounted for two of the killers—two thugs with faces blackened with burned cork. He learned, too, that the banquet victims had been identified— and that each had been a member of Scarborough's grand jury.

Once more, the master of the scarred hand had dealt swift and terrible punishment to the grand jurymen who dared cross him!

But who could that criminal genius be? Corbin had been on the verge of divulging a name when death had closed his lips.

Egel— That sounded like Egelhart, the first assistant district attorney of Queens County, the man who had prosecuted Ownie Garlauf—and stepped out of the way just in time to miss the deadly hail that cut down the jurymen and his own associates....

Thoughtfully, Wentworth bent over the body of Red Corbin and went through his pockets. He found a notebook that gripped his attention, immediately. It contained a list of names and addresses, together with dates. Two of those cryptic notations interested him in particular. One bore the next day's date—and beside it were the names of the mayor and the Queens County district attorney, and the initials N.V.S. Nita van Sloan's initials!

The other was Stud Rickert's name and the present date, the address of a well-known East Side barroom. "Coming-out party" was written beside it. Stud Rickert—the thug who had shot down a defenseless storekeeper for trying to save his property, and then been turned loose by a terrorized jury! This was to have been a brazen celebration of his outrageous acquittal!

STUD RICKERT gulped his beer and loudly demanded another. This was the most successful beefsteak party of his career. The back room of Lannigan's bar and grill had been facetiously decorated to resemble a court of justice, and, propped up on the makeshift bench at one side, was a grinning effigy of Judge Davis in a black cotton robe.

The fifty celebrators who jammed the place were gorged with steak and now amusing themselves by throwing meat and rolls at the inane-looking dummy. Roars of laughter greeted every successful shot, but when Stud stood up at the head of the table his face was stern with mock-seriousness.

"He's had 'nough to eat," he reproved his admirers. "Y'oughta be more c'nsid'-rate. Poor devil must be thirsty—it's hot down in hell where he is now."

A trifle unsteadily, he walked across the room and climbed up on the "bench" with a sloshing glass of beer. Solicitously, he held the dummy's head while he poured the foaming beverage over its face. Grinning with appreciation of his own cleverness, he turned to the applauding spectators. Then his jaw sagged; his mouth hung open and his eyes bulged as if he were looking at a ghost.

And that was what he was staring at!

There, in the side doorway, stood Irving Fisher, the Bronx shoe-store man, his face a sickly grayish white, blood running down from his bashed skull, where Rickert had clubbed him with the automatic barrel, and dripping from the powder-blackened hole in his temple where Rickert had pressed the muzzle of the weapon and sent an unnecessary bullet into his brain!

The beer glass dropped from Stud's hand, crashed to the floor as he gaped at that impossible apparition. Deathly silence gripped the crowded room—and then Stud Rickert reacted in the only way he knew. His hand leaped to his shoulder holster—but before he could make his draw there was another figure beside Fisher—a bent, crouching figure in a long, black cape and floppy, wide-brimmed black hat that only partly concealed a face so ugly that it must belong to the Devil himself!

Rickert's mouth went dry, and his tongue glued to his palate.

His hands were trembling, icy fear creeping up his legs, paralyzing him. Dimly he heard someone yell, "The Spider!" Faintly, he heard the uproar that suddenly broke loose. Desperately, he got his gun out and triggered it madly, blazed away blindly until an agony that was like hell's own ordeal burst in his brain—and after that Stud Rickert was no more.

Before Rickert's body had reached the floor, the Spider was leaping toward it. Now a dozen guns were out, lancing shots at him, but the thunder of his twin automatics sent Stud's outraged followers scurrying to the protection of overturned tables.

For a moment, the Spider swooped over the fallen killer, touched his face. Then his guns were blasting a way back to the side door, where Jackson, in the ghostly masquerade, stood ready to leap into the waiting car and drive away.

Sprawled on the floor of that travesty of a courtroom lay three of Stud Rickert's cronies who had joined him in, death. And plainly printed on his forehead was a small, blood-red replica of a spider—a warning to the underworld and its new master that the Spider was still collecting society's debts!

CHAPTER 6
INNOCENT ABROAD

COMMISSIONER KIRKPATRICK hardly glanced at the latest batch of newspapers dropped on his desk. A glance was all that was necessary to read those screaming black headlines. Every word of the stories that flowed on endlessly beneath them was burned into his reeling brain. Never could he hope to escape them:

"Six Grand Jurors Slain... Stud Rickert Killed... Seven Die in Night Club Slaughter... Four Dead in Barroom Battle Death... Stuns Grand Jury... Spider Avenges Judge Davis." Headline after headline screamed the news of the massacre in the Wee Hours with one breath, the killings in Lannigan's bar with the next. Death in high society and low—and all beating back upon Stanley Kirkpatrick in a deluge of criticism and stinging abuse!

The editorials were worse than the headlines. They damned the police, demanding the commissioner's removal, called on the governor to intervene. One sarcastic diatribe suggested that a vigilante committee be formed with the Spider at its head!

All morning, Kirkpatrick had been trying to get Richard Wentworth on the phone, but always the answer was the same: "Mr. Wentworth isn't in, sir. We haven't heard from him since you called. I don't know when he'll be back. I'll see that he gets your message."

Wentworth was deliberately avoiding him. His servants had relayed to him the commissioner's demand that he give himself up, and this was his answer—disappearance. That slaughter in Lannigan's place last night—that was his answer, too.

Kirkpatrick's eyes glinted with involuntary satisfaction as he thought of the way Stud Rickert had been dealt with, and then clouded as his jaw squared. The Spider had done a job there—and another in the case of Ownie Garlauf—that he would cheerfully have given a year of life to have been able to chalk up to the credit of the police department. Nevertheless, he could not tolerate it. As police commissioner, he could not permit such an outrageous assumption of power by any individual, no matter what the motives.

On the other hand, he was stunned by the complete breakdown of the due legal processes. Never, in his wildest nightmares, could he have imagined anything like this. Yet here it was actually happening. Right out there in the city that stretched beyond his windows a terrible organized army of crime was being created, scoffing at the police, secure in its immunity to law.

Already, the repercussions were being felt in other cities where similar outbreaks were occurring. Or, were these all part of a gigantic crime empire which planned to envelop the whole nation? Again Kirkpatrick's thoughts flashed to the Spider—and suspicion flared high.

It would take the brain of a Spider to conceive such an audacious scheme. It would take the personality of a Spider to put it over; the prestige of a Spider to hold its lawless followers in line. The Spider had killed Garlauf and Rickert—which seemed contradictory if he was the directing genius behind the criminal reign of terror—but the commissioner had profound respect for the Spider's mentality and was perfectly willing to credit him with devious motives that might even seem to conflict....

"Mayor Wallace," Kirkpatrick's secretary announced—and the commissioner hardly dared to meet the eyes of the man who had been his staunch friend for years.

"What are we going to do about it, Kirk?" Wallace waved to the array of newspapers as he sank into a chair. "Never in the

history of the city has the police department been so helpless, so utterly unable to meet a crisis—"

"I'll write out my resignation," Kirkpatrick said wearily.

"So that I can tear it up," the mayor snapped at him. "I don't want your resignation, Kirk; I want your help. Nobody could

handle this job any better than you. I'll stick with you no matter how loud they howl for your scalp. But unless we break up this thing mighty soon we'll both go down together. The governor—"

"Everybody knows where you stand," Kirkpatrick protested. "You can't be blamed if the courts fall down on you. You've denounced them publicly for the way they're turning criminals loose. You've been urging the citizens to do their duty."

"That's talk—and what they want is action," Wallace shook his head. "I've already been warned unofficially that the governor will have me up on charges unless we put a stop to this lawlessness. We're about at the end of our rope, Kirk. We can't just talk and expect people to lose their lives trying to be good citizens."

And Kirkpatrick knew that he was right. The criminal organization had become so powerful that nobody's life was safe. With the steadily increasing impotence of the police and the courts, nobody knew where to turn for security. With authority tottering, anarchy and chaos would rage overnight....

That, he realized suddenly, was what he had always instinctively feared in the activities of the Spider. That was why he had always opposed the Spider's methods. To his conservative, routine-trained mind, the man was a threat to authority—a menace who might get out of hand and run amuck if the taste of power went to his head.

"But, by God, I'll stop him!" he barked suddenly. "I'll put an end to this whole crime wave. Don't ask me how—I'll handle it in my own way. If I don't get action in any other way, I'll go out and get it myself!"

Then his jaw set.

MAYOR WALLACE seemed rather doubtful, rather puzzled, as he left the office. But he would have been even more surprised had he been able to watch his police commissioner during the next half hour. Once his mind was made up, Kirkpatrick started preparations immediately. First, he summoned Inspector O'Neill, headquarters detective staff.

"I want a stool-pigeon in a hurry, Inspector," he ordered. "Someone who is reliable and has entree in places where we can't go. I want him in an hour, at the most. Whom do you suggest?"

"Rubber Charlie is about the best bet," O'Neill decided after a few moments' thought. "He can get in most anywhere—and he knows we've got enough on him to bounce him up the river any time he doesn't come through. I can have him picked up in half an hour."

"Get him," Kirkpatrick clipped, and then he called in one of the department's most expert make-up men.

"I want you to go to work on me and turn me into a drifter," he instructed. "A shabby down-and-outer who is up against it and ready to tackle anything for a few dollars. Make it good—my life may depend on it."

The make-up man went to work with a will, and, within half an hour, Stanley Kirkpatrick was transformed. His ruddy face was sallow and patchy-looking, lined at the mouth and baggy under eyes heavy and bleary. His well barbered hair was long and straggly, hanging down untidily over grimy ears. Even his hands were subtly changed—greasy, stained, with dirty nails. A soiled shirt with a string of a necktie, a shiny suit ragged at the cuffs and spotted, shoes that were shapeless and run-down at the heels—and the job was finished.

So successful was it that Rubber Charlie did not recognize him, even though he had spent an uncomfortable half-hour in the commissioner's office less than a month before. It was a great compliment.

"All right, Charlie, we're going places," Kirkpatrick told him. "I am your pal, Mike Daley, and you're going to get me into the underworld hang-outs—the lower and tougher the better. No tourist joints—I want to get in where the crooks hang out. No arrests; don't worry about that—just someone I'm looking for. All right, let's go."

If the Spider would not come to him, he was going to the Spider!

IT WAS ten-thirty the morning after his first visit to Baumann's pawnshop before Blinky McQuade returned to complete the deal for the sale of his pearls. Uncle Sam was all ready for him. Spread out on the counter beside him was a morning newspaper, folded to an account of the safe-looting in the apartment of James Hollingshurst.

Young Jimmy had handled the job like an artist, giving the reporters a tale replete with mysterious prowlers, strange telephone calls and all the thrilling adjuncts his fertile mind could concoct.

Uncle Sam shook his head sorrowfully the moment Blinky walked in. Significantly, he glanced at the pencil-outlined account, sighed heavily.

"Stealing," he bemoaned. "Just what I feared when you came to me. Stolen goods—and you expect me to handle them for you. You steal—and I should run the risk of going to jail because you break the law. Stealing is bad business, my boy; nothing good comes of it. I don't like to be mixed up with such things."

"Yeah, I know all that," McQuade grinned. "What'll you give me for the necklace? Where is it, anyway? Get it out."

Sadly, the old man brought the envelope from its back-room hiding-place and slid its contents out into his palm. Appreciatively, he regarded the beautifully matched gems, and his eyes sparkled. He was too consummate an artist to attempt to deprecate them, but his attitude was that of one regretfully forced to decline something on which he had set his heart.

"They're worth five grand," Blinky reminded.

"If you could sell them like an honest man," Uncle Sam readily agreed. "But worth nothing if the police confiscate them. It's risky. Detectives will be combing every shop in the city after that," he nodded to the folded newspaper. "For such business I have no heart. But if you insist that I help you—five hundred dollars. That's all—and I don't care if you take them away."

"You're a robber," Blinky protested. "There's no profit in a deal like that. It ain't worth the trouble—"

"That's just the way it should be," Baumann concurred righteously. "If there was no profit there would be no stealing and no trouble."

But Blinky McQuade hardly heard the unctuous homily. From the moment he stepped into the shop, his eyes had been searching for he knew not what. Suddenly, they stopped—and stared unbelievingly through the hooded glasses. There, on a shelf behind the old man, was a miscellaneous assortment of tagged jewelry. On top of the heap lay a brooch that belonged to Nita—one he had given her, himself!

Then she *had* been there. She had pawned her brooch—or

97

it had been taken away from her… Perhaps removed from her lifeless body!

"That gadget back there," he impulsively pointed to the brooch. "How much you want for that? Gimme a decent price on it, an' we'll make a deal on the necklace."

Baumann glanced behind him.

"That's a pledge," he shook his head. "I only took it in this morning. I couldn't sell it for a year, anyway. But I've got lots of others that might do."

That meant that Nita had been there that morning. She probably was using the brooch as he was using the pearls—to gain old Baumann's confidence. Blinky longed to ask more about the deal, to discover whether Uncle Sam knew where to locate her. But he saw that the old man was peering at him over the top of his glasses with quick suspicion. There was nothing to do but drop the matter and close the deal for the necklace.

Now in good standing with the fence, he would be able to come back at any time. He resolved that Uncle Sam would have a chance to pick up another bargain in the very near future. In some way, he sensed, that pawnshop was tied up with the criminal organization he was fighting. But it would be no easy task to penetrate the old man's canny hypocrisy.

"I don't like such business," Baumann was still protesting, as Blinky pocketed his money and left the shop. "I only do it because somebody else—somebody without a conscience—might tempt you with more money to encourage your stealing."

FROM THE pawnshop, Blinky McQuade made his way to the Bit House, and, as he stepped into the smoky barroom, he glanced around alertly to see whether his entrance had attracted hostile attention. Nobody seemed to take notice of him—but perhaps that was because Balmy, himself, mounted guard at the end of the bar and kept a wary eye open.

Blinky had been there about ten minutes when a warning buzzer sounded beneath the bar, and Balmy's battle-scarred head came up alertly. With surprising speed for a man his weight, he sped across the barroom and took his post at a peep-hole in the blind that covered a front window. After a moment of observation, he whistled softly and beckoned to the others. McQuade secured a position at the edge of a blind, as the others swarmed to the windows. From his vantage point, he saw the familiar figure of Rubber Charlie coming down the street in company with a ragged-looking individual—but the reason for the alarm puzzled him.

As he passed Balmy's lookout at the corner of the block, Rubber Charlie had given him a signal, and the lookout had hurried ahead to ring the warning bell from below. For some reason, Charlie wanted them to get a look at his companion before he and his companion entered....

But they weren't going to come in. They were passing on down the block, instead—and as Blinky McQuade stared at the tall, shabbily dressed individual he was puzzled. Then he became incredulous!

Ordinarily, that warning buzzer was used only to give notice that the police were in the neighborhood, and now he understood why Rubber Charlie had employed it. It was his companion. From what Blinky could see, the man's makeup was perfect—but he would recognize Stanley Kirkpatrick's stride anywhere!

A chill of apprehension coursed down Blinky McQuade's spine. Wandering around among these people, divorced from his desk and his assistants, Kirk was a babe in arms—a lamb to be led to the slaughter!

Balmy was going from one to another, whispering instructions, and several of his customers started for the door. Blinky saw them come out on the street and start in the direction Kirkpatrick had gone. A few moments later, he followed and quickly spotted Rubber Charlie standing on the next corner, apparently debating where to go. The wily stool-pigeon was stalling until the killers had time to close in!

At a safe distance, McQuade followed that trail through the maze of crowded, tenement-lined streets, and before long knew its destination. Charlie was heading for China Sam's opium den and gambling-house, a joint where Kirkpatrick would be absolutely helpless....

NEITHER RUBBER Sam nor his shabby companion were in the gaming-rooms of China Sam's well guarded establishment when Blinky McQuade passed inspection at the door and entered. But he located them in the back room that served as a combination bar-and-club lounging-room for the underworld. Kirkpatrick was standing at the bar, trying his best to appear oblivious of the conversation going on around him—while his eyes surreptitiously took a census of the room.

But while Kirk was appraising his companions, he was

entirely unaware of the danger now surely and slyly creeping up on him.

Blinky's jaw hardened as he saw half a dozen killers making their way to positions from which they could trap Kirk in a deadly cross-fire. They were killers whose eyes already gleamed with blood-lust. At any moment now, the death-trap would be sprung.

Quickly, he made his way to the bar and edged up to Kirkpatrick until he was looking straight into the commissioner's unsuspecting eyes. At that moment, one of the curtained booths, that lined one side of the room, opened and out stepped Denny the Wolf, a slinking, ferret-faced cop-killer whom the police had been seeking for months.

The pupils of Denny's close-set eyes were shrunken to murderous pin-points. His arms, slightly arched backward at the elbows, were poised ready for an instant draw, his face was twisted into a leer. Primed with dope-inspired recklessness, he fairly glided toward his victim.

He was almost up to the bar before the commissioner saw him. Instantly, Kirkpatrick was all policeman, his new role forgotten in his sudden rage at finding himself face to face with this cowardly killer who had cut down three of his men. Kirkpatrick's eyes blazed, his shoulders squaring. One hand slid toward his hip pocket while the other reached out to grab the thug's shoulder.

"Denny—" he started to say. And then all hell seemed to break loose in that Oriental-decorated den.

Denny's eager hands snaked toward his guns, but, before

they were out of their holsters, he staggered back, half-blinded as the contents of Blinky McQuade's whisky glass dashed into his face. With seeming awkwardness, Blinky staggered to one side and lunged into the man beside him so that that individual went reeling in front of the commissioner.

At the same moment, Blinky's automatics barked twice—and the main overhead light went out just as the killer, who was drawing a bead on Kirkpatrick's back, grabbed at his throat and slumped to the floor. The room was in an uproar. Men were shouting and cursing as they tried to get out of the way. Others were pressing forward with unsheathed guns, eager to be in at the kill. Someone howled, "Police!" and the mob surged up to the bar in a murderous rush.

Twice more, Blinky's guns barked, and two more lights against the walls shattered to bits. Now the room was in darkness except for the wavering, amber-colored light from a whisky advertisement on the back bar. Liquid and air bubbles flowed up through tubes shaped into letters like neon lights, and the dim glow reflected from them played weirdly on the savage, snarling faces.

Blinky's guns were swinging up and down like clubs, cracking on heads, smashing into faces, as he desperately fought to stem that mad rush. For a split-second, he glanced behind him, where Kirkpatrick should have been—but the commissioner was not there.

And then Blinky saw him, battering his way through the mob, trying to fight his way to the door and drag the limp form of Denny the Wolf after him! The poor, glorious fool—he hadn't a chance of getting out of that dive himself, much less with a prisoner!

The very moment that McQuade's eyes caught him, a thug leaped on his back and clung there while his fist flailed at Kirkpatrick's face. Blinky's gun barked, and the fellow screamed as he rose almost to his full height in the air and then crashed down on top of his mates. But in the same instant a burly fist caught the commissioner on the side of the head and staggered him—and then a gun barrel came down over his skull.

Blinky saw him go down, and desperation sent him charging forward. Kirk was a stubborn old fool in lots of ways, but he was the salt of the earth. Scum like these were not going to trample him to death!

CHARGING LIKE a bull, Blinky toppled men over right and left. Lashing out on all sides with his automatics, he left a trail of bleeding heads in his wake—bleeding heads that sent the cursing thugs at one another's throats as they grappled and fought blindly in the almost complete darkness. Diving beneath swinging fists, stumbling over rolling, threshing bodies, he managed to reach the spot where Kirkpatrick had gone down. He got one hand in his collar, started to drag him toward the door.

Not toward the front door—that would take him through the gambling-rooms. He knew there wasn't a chance of running that gauntlet—and, besides, he had no desire to close this resort to himself for future visits. So far, in the dim light and confusion, nobody had identified his part in the mêlée.

But there was a door at the rear of this room that opened onto a stairway running down to a back alley—an exit China Sam had thoughtfully provided for his customers in case of trouble, and for his own convenience when it was expeditious to remove the body of one of those customers without danger of being seen by passers-by on the street. If that door wasn't locked....

Blinky was almost up to it, when suddenly it opened and the huge figure of China Sam loomed in the doorway. A sub-machine gun under his arm and a powerful flashlight in his other hand, China Sam was going to put a stop to that riot. But before his eyes were accustomed to the darkness something catapulted out of it and crashed into his chin.

McQuade had put every ounce of his strength into that uppercut, and the big Eurasian crumpled without a sound.

Almost in the same motion, Blinky grabbed Kirkpatrick and dragged him across the threshold, pulled the door shut and turned the key in the lock just as the mob from within hurled themselves against it. With the commissioner's body on his back, he staggered down the stairs and through the alley. He left him propped up against the iron gateway at the street while he ran out and hailed a taxi.

"Hopecrest Apartments," Blinky called to the driver and gave him the address. "I've got a sick man here," he allayed the fellow's curiosity. "Stick to your driving, and make it snappy."

Swiftly, he worked as the cab headed uptown. Kirkpatrick was still unconscious, and it took only a few minutes to remove most of the make-up so that he became recognizable. Then he slipped a glove over the commissioner's right hand—a tight-fitting, flesh-like glove with a lurid scar across its back—and pressed the bottom of his cigarette lighter to its palm before he hailed the driver and directed him to pull up at the curb.

"This is as far as I can go with you," he explained and slipped a bill into the cabbie's hand. "Take him to that address. The doorman there will be expecting him."

Kirkpatrick was beginning to stir, blinking his eyes and grabbing at the side of the cab as it got under way again. In a few minutes he would discover the glove on his hand and the small, blood-red spider in its palm. Gradually, memory of what had happened would come back to him. He would realize that he had the Spider to thank for saving his life—or so, at least, Blinky McQuade hoped.

CHAPTER 7
DEATH MARCH

FROM THE time that Jackson relayed Commissioner Kirkpatrick's ultimatum to him, Richard Wentworth had been officially missing from his apartment. When he did go there it was circumspectly, by means of the garages behind the house and the underground passage and private elevator which he had installed for such emergencies. But at frequent intervals during the day he had been keeping in touch with his men by phone, always hoping for some message from Nita.

After the taxicab had sped away with the reviving police commissioner, he looked for a telephone booth and put through one of his customary calls.

"Mike Fogarty tried to get you twice this afternoon, sir,"

NITA VAN SLOAN

Jackson reported. "He's very anxious to see you. Seems pretty much excited—"

Fogarty—that meant a development in Ed Morgan's case, and perhaps some clue to the whereabouts of Nita and Peggy Dunning....

Blinky hurried to the hide-out garage and divested himself of his make-up. He drove out in his proper Wentworth personality for Fogarty's office—the private investigator had no acquaintance with Blinky McQuade or the Spider. To him, Richard Wentworth was a wealthy young clubman with a penchant for getting himself embroiled in dangerous mix-ups, a well-paying customer whose appearance generally meant plenty of action for Mike Fogarty.

He looked up excitedly the moment Wentworth walked into his little office.

"There's hell to pay in that Morgan case, Mr. Wentworth." His fat face creased in a scowl. "All along, there's been somebody putting pressure on that grand jury. It was only a question of how soon they'd bring in an indictment against him. You knew that—but this afternoon somebody else set them all back on their heels. When they went to the jury-room, after the lunch recess, there was a note propped up on the center table. That note threatened them with all kinds of hell if Ed Morgan is indicted!

"The thing was typewritten and signed with a drawing of a hand with a scar on its back—I found out that much, and that's about all anybody seems to know. How it got there has everybody stumped, and the D. A.'s been raising hell."

A note from the scarred-hand organization? But Wentworth knew at once that the thing was a fake. It was the scarred-hand outfit that was railroading young Morgan, bringing threatening pressure to bear so that he would be indicted and sent to

the electric chair as a punishment for killing Ruigi. This note was a desperate attempt to block them—and he didn't need two guesses to tell who had sent it.

Peggy Dunning had seen that scarred-hand signature on the threatening note she received. She and Nita were taking a hand in the game, fighting the master criminal with his own weapon of intimidation....

"Where's that note now, Fogarty?" he clipped suddenly.

"In the D.A.'s safe over in Long Island City, I suppose." Fogarty ran his fingers through a sparse fringe of reddish hair. "Of course, if I'd a-known you wanted to see it—"

"You're getting to be a mind-reader, Mike," Wentworth ignored the sarcasm. "That's just what I do want—and what I'm *going* to do. *Now*—as fast as I can drive over to Queens. You seem to know your way around pretty well over there. How about coming along?"

Fogarty's hands were clasped over his big paunch as he rocked back in his swivel-chair. For a moment, he poised in mid-air and his heavy, double-chinned jaw dropped open with surprise.

"That will be breaking—" he started, and then shrugged ponderously as he heaved his bulk out of the protesting chair. "Come on, I'm game. I'd sort of like to get one look at that note myself."

THEY DIDN'T actually have to break in when they reached the courthouse in Long Island City. Fogarty scouted around the building and soon located a lower door used by cleaning women and the janitor. It was unlocked, and they stepped inside without being seen, cautiously cat-footing their way up to the floor on which the district attorney's office was located. The corridors were dark and utterly still—not a light or a sound until they were almost to their objective—but there *was* someone in the D.A.'s office. Light shone through the glass panel, and a low murmur of voices came through the partly-opened transom.

Wentworth crept close to the door, and Fogarty was right behind him as he peered through the keyhole. It was blocked. There was no other way of getting a look into that office, unless he could get a grip on the edge of the transom....

"Here," Fogarty whispered, and held out his finger-locked hands to serve as a boost.

From the edge of the transom, Wentworth stared into the office—stared at the frowning face of First Assistant District Attorney Martin Egelhart as he bent over his desk, his head close to that of Herman Spiegelman, of the New York County D. A.'s office. They were intently studying a typewritten note, comparing it with another specimen of typewriting.

"Of course, it's not the same," Spiegelman said with obvious relief as he straightened up. "I knew that it couldn't be—but I don't like it, Martin." His voice filled with concern. "Whoever sent it knows—"

He stopped when he saw Martin Egelhart grinning triumphantly.

"I happen to know who sent it," Egelhart sprang his surprise as he reached down and took two other letters from a desk drawer. "Take a look at these. This one we received from Miss Nita van Sloan about the Morgan case. You will notice that it is written on the same distinctive stationery as the threatening note. Now have a look at this one—from Peggy Dunning, Morgan's fiancée, protesting our keeping him locked up. The handwriting is identical with the corrections written into our note. Not a question in the world that they sent it."

"So Morgan's girl and Nita van Sloan are trying to bulldoze the grand jury!" Spiegelman whistled with surprise and satisfaction. "That means you can pick them up—"

"I could if I wanted to—yes," Egelhart nodded significantly. "But I hardly think that will be necessary."

Richard Wentworth was amazed—not at learning that the girls had sent the threatening note, but at the perfectly obvious slip-ups they had made in doing it. In her excitement, Peggy Dunning might have made such blunders, but Nita....

And then, suddenly, he understood. These apparent slips were intentional! They had been made deliberately so that the identity of the writers would become known! Nita and Peggy Dunning wanted the man who was trying to railroad Ed Morgan to the electric chair to find them. They were offering themselves as bait to make him reveal himself—putting themselves in deadly peril to accomplish their purpose!

"These meddlers can be taken care of a great deal more easily, if we let them run loose," Egelhart was saying. "In jail is just the place where I don't want them."

But to jail was just the place where they were going, Wentworth vowed grimly as he clung to the transom ledge. He would order Fogarty to use every means to see to it that they were apprehended. He would instruct him to tell District Attorney Cunnison what they had discovered, and have him insist the girls be jailed for attempting to influence the grand jury. Jail was the safest place for them—as long as he could not locate and take them under his own protection.

MARTIN EGELHART was a cautious talker, but, as he listened, Wentworth realized the extent and power of the criminal organization he was fighting. It had wormed its way into the offices of at least two of the city's five county district attorneys—there was no way of telling how much deeper into the municipal administration.

Fogarty was grunting low-voiced protests as he tried to keep his locked hands together. But suddenly Wentworth tensed, straining to catch every word of the low-voiced conversation within that office.

"You're sure Baldwin will be there?" Egelhart was asking.

"He wouldn't miss it for the world," Spiegelman grinned. "Wallace and Baldwin and Cunnison—all at one sweep!"

Wallace, the mayor; Baldwin, the New York County district attorney; Cunnison, the D.A. from Queens....

"And I think we're going to have the pleasure of entertaining Brother Thompson, from Brooklyn," Egelhart chuckled. "His wife is such a social climber that she won't let him miss an opportunity to shine at the swanky Oak Hills Club. Man, this will be a night little old Great Neck will remember!" He glanced at his watch. "They should all be there by now—all set for the fireworks!"

Andrew Thompson, the Kings County district attorney... Three district attorneys and the mayor... Wentworth's nerves quivered with excitement as he groped for a significance that perversely eluded him—and then he had it! The notation in Red Corbin's notebook! The memorandum with the mayor's name and Nita's initials and today's date—this was the *place* to go with that date—the ultra-fashionable Oak Hills Country Club in Great Neck!

The mayor and the district attorneys were to be there tonight—were there now—and Nita would be there, too! "All at one sweep... A night little old Great Neck will remember... All set for the fireworks..." Those phrases rang ominously in his ears as he released his grip on the transom edge and grasped Fogarty's shoulders.

Wentworth whispered grimly as he started down the hall-way, "Unless I miss my hunch, the fate of the New York City administration may hang on what we do in the next hour," and he proceeded to tell Fogarty everything.

"We could phone out there and warn them," the detective considered.

"And be taken for a couple of nuts!" Wentworth clipped. "They wouldn't believe us. Even if they did, warning them might be just the spark to set off the explosion."

"Maybe we better go to the police?"

"And tell them that we broke into the courthouse to spy on the district attorney's men?" Wentworth jeered. "We'd land in a pair of cells. Even if the police paid any attention to our tale, by the time they took action it would be too late. Besides, we can't run the chance that there may be disaffected men at police headquarters just as there are in the district attorneys' offices. That would be fatal. We're going out to Great Neck as fast as we can get there. That's the only thing we can do, Mike. And you might do a little praying that we don't get there too late!"

He moved forward.

CAUTIOUSLY, THEY darted from the building and climbed into Wentworth's car. In the next half hour the powerful motor under the commonplace-looking hood raced at top speed as they sped toward Great Neck. As they turned into the spacious grounds of the Oak Hills Club, they saw the lights of the clubhouse twinkling through the trees ahead of them and the ranks of automobiles in the parking-space at the rear. But before they could reach it Wentworth jammed his foot on the brake.

Stretched across the driveway, blocking it completely, was a wooden horse with *No Admittance* painted on its cross-bar.

Wentworth tensed and peered out into the darkness. His hand darted to the switch, snapped off the lights. Out there beside the road he heard a footstep, saw a dark shadow coming toward the car.

"Watch yourself!" he whispered to Fogarty. "This looks like a trap."

The big detective already had the door on his side of the car opened. The car lurched as he stepped on the running-board. Then a hand swept in through Wentworth's window, lashed out viciously at his head as the square of lighter darkness was blotted out by a burly figure that clung to the windshield post and groped for the door handle.

Instinctively, Wentworth slumped, flattening himself against the bottom of the seat just as something thudded against the rear cushion. His hand swung up, to bring the barrel of his automatic crashing down on a head dimly discernible above the wheel. The fellow groaned as the breath soughed out of his lungs. His hand dropped down onto the wheel, lay there a second, and then slipped back out of the window as his body collapsed and tumbled off the running-board.

In the same instant, Wentworth pushed himself across the seat and out of the door after Fogarty. The big fellow was cursing softly as his huge fists smacked against a face now almost on top of him and grabbed an attacker with both hands, swept him off his feet, and heaved him into a clump of bushes. With a bellow of rage he whirled on another fellow clinging to his back—but the shout died, half-uttered, as a blackjack thudded sickeningly down on his skull.

Wentworth heard that crack, and, in the next moment, exacted swift vengeance as the barrel of one of his automatics bit down through flesh and bone. The thug who had been thrown into the brush was now getting to his feet, branches snapping and crackling under his weight. Before he was free of them, Wentworth's fist drove into his belly and then swung up mightily under his unprotected jaw.

After that—silence.

The whole struggle had taken little more than a minute, and

evidently had attracted no attention except from the three who had been posted there in the driveway. For a split-second, Wentworth hesitated; then he chanced a ray of light from his pencil-flash. Fogarty was unconscious, blood running down his head where the blackjack had hit him. But Wentworth's exploring fingers could feel no broken bone. The man should be taken to a doctor, but that would have to wait.

Straining, tugging, Wentworth heaved the bulky body back into the car, closed the door. Then he glanced at the three who had waylaid them. One seemed to be dead, and the other two would be unconscious for quite a while. All three wore dark suits and soft hats pulled low over their foreheads. Quickly, he stripped off one's coat and hat, donned them.

Then he started cautiously through the bushes toward the clubhouse. The sound of music was plain and the lights were brighter, but there seemed to be nobody around outside the building. Then he almost stumbled headlong over a body lying beside a clump of evergreens. The body was that of a uniformed man—the club doorman—blood matting face and neck from a broken head!

The man was dead, needlessly murdered—and Wentworth's lips set as he realized how ruthless were the killers he faced....

CAREFULLY, HE made a circuit of the big building, and, when that was accomplished, the apprehension welling up within him became a cold, clammy thing that clutched at his heart. At no less than four places his keen eyes had spotted men crouched at the low French windows, their sub-machine guns trained on the main dance-floor! One or two of those killers he might be able to surprise and knock out—but the risk was too great. If he failed—if his blow was not sufficiently sure and the fellow had a chance to pull the trip on his deadly gun—nothing would be able to halt the fearful slaughter that must begin!

Four murderous killers at their posts—and at least one who was coordinating and directing them. Wentworth drew back barely in time as the fellow loomed up ahead, gliding to the nearest of his men.

"The grand march will be next," came the hoarse whisper. "Remember, wait until they come down the hall eight abreast. Then let 'em have it!"

A nod of understanding from the crouching gunman, and the leader's dark figure merged with the shadow, to carry his message to the next outpost of death.

The grand march! Wentworth pressed close against one of the windows and peered into the brightly lighted ballroom. At one end of the hall the merrymakers were already lining up, laughing and jesting, wholly unaware of the ghastly doom that hung over them. Up at the head of the forming line of couples, Wentworth recognized the three district attorneys with their wives. Mayor Wallace was coming to the front—at his side Nita van Sloan!

Realization smashed home into Wentworth's stunned brain. Nita was at the dance, alone. Probably, she had intended to come with Red Corbin—that would explain her initials in his notebook. But, since her intended escort was eliminated, she had come by herself. She was an intimate friend of Mayor Wallace and his family. What more natural than that he should ask her to lead the march with him?

That gay march would start with couples, double to fours, to eights—then, as it swept across the hall, a deadly hail of machine-gun bullets would batter it from four points! The mayor, district attorneys, judges and other prominent persons in the second and third rows would be cut down in the most ghastly massacre on record in New York City!

Nita was curtsying to Mayor Wallace, as he bowed and offered her his arm. The musicians were taking their places on the orchestra dais, picking up their instruments....

Richard Wentworth now faced the greatest emergency of his entire career. He was helpless. Nothing he could do would stop this fearful carnage about to commence. Anything he might attempt would only precipitate it. Any move he made not only would forfeit his own life but would also unleash a death-torrent upon those unsuspecting marchers. Anything—

But there was *one* desperate possibility!

To attempt to effect this meant sacrificing his own life, but it might succeed in staving off the leaden hail until the others could run to safety—and Nita was snatched from death. But, if he accomplished that, the Spider would not have died for nothing....

THE OPENING strains of the grand march were ringing in his ears, the picture of Mayor Wallace and Nita smilingly leading the procession was dancing before his eyes, as Wentworth slipped away from the window, sped back to his car. Feverishly, he went to work with his make-up box. Never before had the ugly features of the Spider taken form so quickly beneath his skillful fingers.

In an incredibly short time a twisted, black-caped figure darted from the car and ran back to the clubhouse. Then the Spider's heart contracted as he peered through one of the windows. *The marchers had already executed the preliminary circling of the hall!* Mayor Wallace was leading the way toward the end opposite the orchestra, and the floor manager was all ready to start them down through the center of the room in the first of the final maneuvers!

Once before, Wentworth had been inside that clubhouse. On his memory of the layout of the place, the success of his desperate stratagem must depend. If he could get into a cellar window... At the rear he found one that yielded to his eager fingers. Now the stairs that led up to the dressing-rooms behind the little stage must be over there at the farther side... It was! With pounding heart, he sped up the steps, reached out for the doorknob. It turned. The door opened, swung inward with the slightest creaking noise!

It was enough to attract the attention of the man who stood at the switchboard panel, ready to operate the lights. Wonder-ingly, he turned around—then almost collapsed at sight of the twisted, stooping figure scuttling through the doorway!

Instantly, the Spider was at his side, one warning hand order-ing silence while the other held him fast. Through the little opening beside the panel, Wentworth looked out into the hall. The marchers were sweeping across the hall in a column of fours, to be divided at the upper end and started back for the next fatal doubling that would bring them up eight abreast!

"Listen to me!" his voice firm, authoritative, that of one who must be obeyed. "Death is going to sweep that hall and turn this place into a shambles in the next two or three minutes. We are surrounded by killers. The mayor, district attorneys, everyone will be mowed down. You and I are the only ones who can stop it, do you understand? You and the Spider!

"I'm going out there to draw their fire. The minute I leap out on that floor, I want you to put out all the lights and turn on the revolving chandelier. After that, you will use your own judgment. The longer I stay on my feet the better chance we'll have of saving dozens of lives."

The two columns of fours were meeting at the foot of the hall, merging into a column of eight marching forward amid an outburst of applause—when suddenly the lights blotted out. A strange, blood-curdling sound rang through the ballroom—the sound of a man's laughter so weird and horrible that it clutched at throats, froze blood in veins!

Before its cackling echo had died away, the big crystal-and-mirror chandelier in the room's center began to turn, bathing the place in mottled specks of illumination as concealed lights played upon it. Directly beneath it cavorted a bent, twisted creature—the embodiment of all evil suddenly spawned from the depths of hell itself!

"Down! Down on the floor! Down on your faces, if you want to live!" the Spider shouted as he gyrated like a monstrous top. His twin automatics blazed straight at the marchers, but just over their heads. "Down or you'll die where you stand!"

WEIRD, WILDLY fantastic, terrifying was that mad dance in the flickering light, with bursts of orange flame flashing in

119

the darkness. Utterly astounding paralyzing—but it could not last. The Spider leaped to one side just as a machine gun started to chatter at one of the windows. Another echoed it; another! He leaped wildly into the air, darted back and forth like a cat on a hot stove, flung himself flat on the floor—then, suddenly, the lights seemed to have gone even crazier than he! White, red, blue, green, yellow—flashing and flickering in a blinding display the spectacle rivaled the aurora borealis!

Nobody could see in that crazy torrent of light and the Spider fervently gave thanks for the man at that light panel. He was a genius, an inspired marvel! Nobody could see—but the Spider didn't have to see. He knew where those gunners were concealed the blaze of flame from the gun-muzzles was there to direct his aim.

Never in his life had he shot more carefully or effectively. One of those guns was no longer blazing. A strangled scream from the other side of the room told him that another killer had been eliminated from this ghastly game. Deliberately he crouched, emptied both barrels at the spot from which a third gun was chattering.

Three guns had been silenced—and that whirling dervish who had sprung out onto the floor to give up his life that others might live was still incredibly alive, still swooping, pirouetting. One more gun now. The Spider started toward it, his guns vomiting flame as he darted from side to side....

But that gunner did not wait to meet him. He had seen what had happened to three of his mates, and now this impossible killer—this creature who couldn't be downed—was coming for him! With a yell of terror, the assassin bolted, his useless weapon clattering out onto the dance floor!

Silence came then—after that thunderous noise almost shocking. Suddenly, the bright lights flashed on and revealed a dance-floor covered with prone men and women who seemed trying to burrow down into the very wood itself for protection. Living men and women dead now but for a miracle that they would never quite understand.

For a long moment, the Spider was the only one there on his feet. Then, the danger past, men started springing up. Hysterical bedlam broke loose. Nita was up with the others now, trying desperately to race out to the Spider—*but* the mayor had his arms around her, holding the girl as he fought to calm her.

With a wave of his hand that he knew she would understand, the Spider dived out of an open window and raced for his car. Fogarty must be rushed to a doctor without further delay; already the wounded man had too long gone unattended.

CHAPTER 8
DUST TO DUST

NITA VAN SLOAN was crestfallen, discouraged, as she rode back to Manhattan in the mayor's car, scarcely listening as he marveled over their miraculous escape from death. She had counted so much on this evening. But it had turned out as unproductive of anything tangible as all other leads followed in this strange crime drama.

Almost as soon as she had become involved with Peggy

Dunning, and set out to discover who it was that directed the gigantic crime campaign that had ridden roughshod over the girl and her brother, Nita had remarked Red Corbin's prominence in the criminal picture. Just as, unknown to herself, Richard Wentworth had reacted to Corbin's activity, she had sensed that it was more than coincidence, or even newspaper ability, that made the feature writer so ubiquitous when sensational trouble broke.

Deliberately, she had set out to investigate Corbin. After she managed to meet him through a common friend, she had cultivated him carefully, playing up to him like a celebrity-worshiping society girl.

"You must have that nose for news so important to a real newspaperman, Mr. Corbin!" she had flattered him. "You are always there ahead of the others. Your stories are so much more vivid and colorful. You always make me feel as if I were right there, seeing the thing happen. It must be *thrilling* to actually *be* there and see such astonishing things with your own eye!"

Red Corbin fell for it—just as many a shrewder man had capitulated when Nita van Sloan turned her lovely eyes upon him, weaving spells around him with the soft magic of her vibrant voice. He impulsively offered to take her to the Oak Hills Club dance.

Instinctively, she had known that this was to be no mere routine society function. She had sensed that she was on the trail of something important—finally to have her hopes shattered when Red Corbin was killed the night before the dance. Yet, so strong was her hunch that she decided to use the invitation

Corbin had sent her, even though that meant going unescorted. Only in that way could she get closer to the arch-criminal Dick Wentworth was fighting—the man against whom he preferred to carry on single-handedly, spurning her assistance.

Her hunch had been right—but instead of accomplishing anything, her blundering effort had almost cost her life, and Dick's as well.

Yet, as she reviewed the debacle, there lingered one dim ray of hope. The evening's events had thrust her even more prominently into the limelight—so prominently that the master-criminal surely must make a direct bid for her now....

MAYOR WALLACE drove her to her apartment, but, as soon as his car had disappeared, she stepped back into the street and hailed a taxi, going to the Claremore Hotel. Peggy Dunning had been there alone all evening, and, in her distraught condition, there could be no telling what the worried girl might be doing. However, with relief Nita found her asleep when she softly let herself into Peggy's room.

She went into the adjoining room which she had engaged for herself and plugged in a small, portable radio, preparing for bed. As she suspected, the sensational attack on the mayor occupied all the newscasters, and bulletin after bulletin interrupted the music programs.

"From the electrician of the Oak Hills Club it has been definitely established that the man who thwarted this attempt on the mayor's life claimed to be the Spider," a sonorous voice announced as she dozed off to sleep. "Without his intervention, it is probable that hundreds of men and women would have been

The Spider's guns cleared
the plot in record time.

shot down. Again the Spider seems to have stepped in at the crucial moment and thwarted what otherwise would have been an unthinkable atrocity. Again he has performed a public service that should have been handled by the police—"

Sleepily, she reached out, silenced the instrument. But when she opened her eyes again, in the morning, it seemed as if that long-winded voice had gone right on speaking through the night.

"One of the most prompt consequences of the attempted assassination of the mayor last evening was the action taken by the Queens County grand jury this morning," the announcer was saying. "For several days, this grand jury has been considering the indictment of Ed Morgan for the slaying of Joe Ruigi, an armed housebreaker, during a hold-up in the Richmond Hill home of the late Philip Dunning, even though District Attorney Cunnison has strongly advised against such action. Convening at an unusually early hour this morning, the grand jury promptly indicted Morgan for first-degree murder—"

A shocked gasp brought Nita bolt upright in bed. There, on a chair in front of the radio, was Peggy Dunning, staring into the cloth-covered speaker with wild, frenzied eyes.

"They've indicted him!" she chattered. "You heard it? They'll murder him, just as surely as they murdered Phil! They'll drag him into court and put him on trial—and if the terrified jury doesn't convict him they will be shot down just as Phil was. Oh, he hasn't got a chance—and he didn't do it! I'm going to tell them! I can't let this go on any longer! I won't let them drag him to his death—"

Then Nita had the sobbing girl in her arms.

"You won't help him a bit that way," she reminded. "We've been all over that, Peggy. There is nothing to be gained by rushing out with hysterical stories that nobody will believe. This indictment will mean nothing if our plan succeeds. It hasn't failed—yet. We won't give up hope—not until after this afternoon, anyway. Now, pull yourself together. We're going to your brother's funeral this afternoon, just as we've been planning. You mustn't let yourself go to pieces."

Peggy Dunning tremblingly promised, but now Nita looked forward to the coming ceremony with more than misgivings....

EXCEPT FOR the curious crowd that jammed the sidewalk outside the house, and a number of policemen on hand to keep order, there seemed to be nothing unusual about the Dunning funeral. Carefully, Nita scrutinized each guest who arrived for the quiet home ceremony. But with the exception of herself and a number of newspapermen, all who came in were relatives or close friends of the family.

There was nothing out of the ordinary—and yet she could not believe that the criminal dictator would allow this occasion to pass unnoticed. It was too fine an opportunity to mete out spectacular punishment to her and Peggy Dunning for daring to oppose him.

Alert, ready for any emergency, she sat through the service, while her heart went out for Peggy's grief. But there had been no disturbance, by the time the casket was closed and borne from the house—nothing when she stepped into a motor-coach beside Peggy, and the cortège got under way.

As the procession rolled on to the cemetery, Nita kept constant vigil behind the drawn blinds of the coach. Yet nothing untoward occurred to mar the trip. At one point, she noticed that the hearse got ahead of the coaches, separated from them by a red light and heavy traffic, speeding on apparently without a realization of what had happened. By the time the light had changed, it had disappeared, and the puzzled drivers held council before proceeding. However, they decided to go on to the cemetery. A short while later, they caught up with the hearse where it was idling along, waiting.

That left only the brief service at the grave—and Nita's pulse quickened with excitement. Posted unobtrusively around the burial plot, as soon as they stepped out of the coach and approached it, were what appeared to be uniformed policemen and detectives. Instinctively, she did not trust them. She noted how ceaselessly their eyes followed Peggy and herself.

There was something about those men, their carriage, faces....

Peggy Dunning sensed it, too. Nita felt the girl's fingers clutching her sleeve, digging into her arms. Then her frightened whisper, "Those men—who are they, Nita?"

"Police," Nita tried to quell her panic. "They've been stationed here, just in case of trouble. There's nothing to worry about—"

"But the one over there near that monument," Peggy's voice shook with terror. "I'm sure he was one of the men who robbed our house. He was the one who came running downstairs—Oh, God, Nita, he sees that I recognize him—he's coming toward us!"

Nita had seen the guards drawing closer, converging on

her and Peggy. She had noticed something else, too. One of those who had remained in the background, but was now coming forward was the thug whose hand  she had bitten when he was torturing Peggy in the room behind Sam Baumann's pawnshop! She had caught a glimpse of him, as she stepped out of the coach, and thought that she recognized him. Now there could be no mistake.

His hands were thrust into the pockets of his topcoat, ugly face set, expectant. For an instant, she caught the flash of dark eyes that were sardonic, triumphant. Like a net, he and his fellows were closing in—with nobody to halt them.

"Quiet!" she whispered desperately, as she squeezed Peggy's wrist until the pressure hurt. "Not a sound!"

If the terrified girl screamed, the sound of her voice would be the signal to start a score of deadly guns blazing. It would send the helpless mourners toppling into the newly made grave waiting to receive the corpse of Phil Dunning. Nita could make out the outlines of weapons in the coat pockets—wary muzzles covering all of the little funeral party and almost upon her and the shivering girl.

Now the hearse was drawn up a short distance from the plot,

doors open, casket being lifted to the pallbearers' shoulders. This would be the moment! When every eye was concentrated upon that approaching casket, she and Peggy would suddenly be seized....

Sharp and shrill, a high-pitched whistle cut through her thoughts and snapped the tense spell that gripped her. Then, astoundingly, the top of the casket flew open. While the stupefied pallbearers stood rooted to the ground like graven images, hardly daring to swivel their eyes to the incredible thing that was happening up there on their shoulders, the casket pitched slightly forward—and out of it sprang a scowling, gargoyle-faced creature in a long black cape and wide-brimmed hat!

With blazing guns, the Spider leaped from his strange bed. For a moment, he poised there above the heads of the astonished funeral party, while his bullets raked the converging killers. Then, as the thugs rallied from their amazement, he scrambled to the ground and started toward them.

LIKE A huge, misshaped black crab, he scurried across the burial plot, now abruptly cleared of the wildly fleeing mourners; and the courage seeped out of the gun-brave killers when that baleful Nemesis bore down on them. Panic-stricken, they took to their heels, flinging themselves down behind the protection of granite monuments or railing posts. Even from that sanctuary, their aim was ineffective, for discouragingly accurate bullets lanced down at them from the roof of the hearse, where its driver lay flattened.

The Spider's guns cleared the plot of thugs in record time. Cursing and moaning, they writhed on the ground, or sprawled out in the stillness that would be theirs for all time, as he pressed relentlessly on toward the struggling group which had been his focal point from the moment he rose in the casket. Nita and Peggy Dunning were in the center of the group, so entwined with vicious-faced hoodlums, who were trying to force them back toward the roadway, that the Spider did not dare shoot.

Grimly, he cut down the distance between them, seemingly impervious to the wild bullets hastily triggered at him. Ugly face distorted into a mask of hatred, he leaped in to close with them—when suddenly the graveyard was filled with blue-coated men who seemed to rise out of the ground itself!

From all sides, the police charged out of the ambush that had concealed them so effectively that their presence had not even been suspected. Before the Spider could whirl and confront this new menace, a nightstick glanced off his head and almost stretched him senseless. Dazed, he staggered backward and reached out vainly for something to grasp, cling to, until his head had a chance to clear.

His groping hands clutched emptiness. He was falling, going down... Then he was picked up almost bodily by the uniformed driver and rushed to where the hearse stood with its motor still running.

"Hold on!" Jackson panted. "We're moving fast!"

With a wild lurch, the car was under way, swinging out of the driveway while bullets shattered its windows and sang past the driver's seat. Picking up speed, it raced down the cemetery road, headed for the hill that led to the entrance. The Spider's head had been clearing rapidly. Now the excitement of the chase swept the last trace of dizziness from his brain. It brought home to him the realization that he was leaving Nita behind to her fate. He was helpless to go to her aid!

"We can't get far in this outfit," he decided quickly. "I'm getting out. No—don't slow up—you haven't a second to lose. I'll jump."

Crazily, the hearse sailed around a turn and careened down the steep grade of the hill. Jackson clung to the wheel, not daring to take his eyes off the road. Behind him, he heard the wail of police sirens. The door at the other side of the seat clicked open, and he deliberately cut in close to the shrub-lined side of the road.

"Luck!" he yelled—and then the seat beside him was empty. The Spider was hurtling through the air, to land in the leaf-piled ditch, roll like a ball before he could regain his feet, then dart down a narrow, mausoleum-lined cemetery street.

ONE AFTER the other, the Spider tried the metal doors until he located one that opened to the turned handle. In the chilly, semi-dark interior he found a pile of old wreaths and set-pieces, long since faded and desiccated but still furnishing ideal covering.

Quickly, his trained fingers went to work, and soon the repellent features of the Spider began to disappear, transformed into the weak, perpetually scowling face of Blinky McQuade. The black cape and hat folded up into a flat bundle, and out of another pocket came a battered thing of soiled felt that soon took shape as Blinky's nondescript headpiece.

Two leads were open to him, he considered, as he made his

way toward the cemetery gates—Sam Baumann's pawnshop and Martin Egelhart, first assistant district attorney of Queens County. The district attorney would be the harder nut to crack but if he could put the pressure on Uncle Sam....

AS UTTERLY amazed as any of the mourners, Nita van Sloan had stared, thunderstruck, when the lid of Phil Dunning's coffin flew back and the Spider erupted from it. But only for a moment. Then wild elation surged through her.

Dick had come for her!

Peggy screamed wildly—and Nita saw the girl struggling in the hands of two of the devils. They were dragging her toward the road. Nita broke away from the men who had grabbed her—but, instead of running to Dick for safety, she flung herself at the thugs tugging at Peggy.

In a moment, all of them were inextricably mixed in a wild confusion.

Then her feet were swept from under her. Strong arms seized her and she was picked up bodily, rushed toward the road. A big sedan loomed up, and she was thrust head-first through its open door, to be dumped down on the back seat beside Peggy. Two of the thugs leaped in with them. Another, at the wheel, stepped on the throttle—and the car darted off.

The sedan raced out through the cemetery gates. Suddenly, it skidded to one side and seemed on the point of overturning as the driver jammed on the brakes to avoid colliding with another car that came flashing down the avenue. The abrupt stop lifted Nita from the seat, spilled her on the floor—and then her quick wit snatched at the opportunity.

As she slipped from the seat, she grabbed at the door handle, yanked it down, flung the door wide. All in the same motion, her arm closed around the knees of the man with the gun, and, before he could finish his yelp of surprise, he was floundering on the floor with her.

"Jump, Peggy!" she screamed wildly.

For a split-second, wild confusion reigned in the rear of that car. Peggy shrieked and pitched through the doorway. The fellow who had been guarding her cursed and made a desperate snatch for her. He grabbed no more than a piece of her dress that tore loose. It was all.

The startled driver glanced behind him—then stepped on the gas.

"We can't stop now!" he roared.

That was all Nita heard. For an instant, the snarling face of the gunman she had spilled glared down at her. Then his automatic came down over her head.

CHAPTER 9
ONE WHO WAITS

THE EVENING papers were on the stands when Blinky McQuade got back to Manhattan. Newsboys were shouting extras about the cemetery gun-battle, and, in the course of one of these accounts, he found the information he sought. Nita van Sloan and Peggy Dunning had been daringly kidnapped right under the eyes of the police! The Dunning girl had managed to escape and run hysterically into the arms of a policeman near the cemetery gates; but Nita van Sloan had been carried off in an unidentified automobile.

So the cemetery trap had partially succeeded, and this murdering monster, to whom human life meant nothing, had gotten his hands on Nita. He was holding her for God only knew what devilish purpose… That meant that time was short, indeed. Blinky McQuade's scowl had a deeper, grimmer cast as he turned his footsteps toward the Bowery.

Outwardly, the antiquated pawnshop looked as usual when he approached it, but the moment he stepped inside he saw the change. Old Uncle Sam was not behind the counter. In his place was a smooth faced, hawk-nosed young fellow with the beady eyes of a snake.

All the weight of Blinky's perfectly coördinated body was behind the fist that smashed into the hawk-nose and crumpled the cartilage like paper. Then his arms wrapped around the sagging body. They tumbled to the floor behind the counter— just as a storm of lead swept the little shop.

Blinky's spectacled eyes swung to that doorway barely in time to see a sheet of flame jutting from the muzzle of a submachine gun. The deadly muzzle tilted downward, seeking him. Instantly, he fell flat on the floor, grabbing the inert body of the counter-man and twisting it over in front of him with one hand, while the other flashed to his shoulder holster for an automatic that added its savage bark to the deafening din.

The human shield in front of him jerked, quivered, as a stream of bullets tore into it. Blood and particles of flesh spattered him—and then, as if a red-hot iron stabbed through the back of

"So you're the murdering devil behind this reign of terror!"

his left shoulder, the thing lanced its way agonizingly through the flesh!

Queer, unnatural quiet settled over the shop—quiet almost palpable after that fury of riotous fire.

His ears tingled at the first sound. That was the slither of scraping footsteps. In the back room? Someone crawling away—or inching his way back to the fallen Tommy gun?

"He's dead, I tell yuh, Jake," a voice sounded. "Come on—let's get outa here."

But at that moment a sleek-haired head inched cautiously over the edge of the counter close beside one of the showcases. Two narrowed eyes peered down into the shadows—and Blinky McQuade's flaming gun bored a third gaping eye dead-center between them! Every shot was counting.

Before the investigator's body had time to slip back over the counter and slump to the floor, there was a howl of rage from his companions. Several were out there in the shop, darting to cover and sieving the front of the counter with lead—but, the moment his gun blazed, Blinky dived headlong for the curtained doorway.

Nobody disputed his way, and, as he raced through Baumann's humble living-room, he saw the old man lying on the floor. Blood had gushed from a wound in his temple and trickled down his face.

Blinky hesitated for a moment, but there was no time to stop and see whether the pawnbroker still lived. Police whistles were shrilling out in the street.

The place might already be surrounded, but he had to chance

that to find a way out. Trapped here by the police would mean hours of detention, endless questioning and the probable breakdown of his masquerade—with resulting arrest as Richard Wentworth.

BEYOND UNCLE SAM'S living-room, he found a noisome lavatory. Small and narrow, but there was a painted window above the old-fashioned water-closet—large enough for him to creep through if he could get it open. That was hopeless, investigation revealed at once. The window was painted shut, almost cemented into its frame. But if it was not barred on the outside....

Quickly, he turned the key in the lock and leaped up onto the toilet. His automatic shattered the pane and was hammering out the jagged pieces of glass that still clung to the age-old putty when a hand grabbed the doorknob and rattled it.

"Open up in there!" a gruff voice ordered. "Open up, y' hear what I say?"

Blinky was up on the sill, twisting his shoulders through the narrow opening. Only then did he realize the seriousness of his wounds. It was pure hell to move that left shoulder. His fingers were fastened on the outer ledge above the window, clinging to it while he drew his feet clear, when the door rattled and quivered. He dropped a few feet to the back yard, just as it cracked and ripped away.

Those wounds were dangerous, his throbbing shoulder reminded him. Clotted blood had run down his back and glued his shirt to his skin, but every time he moved the wounds opened again, the warm trickle resuming. The shoulder should be dressed without delay, and the nearest place to give it proper attention was his room in Holian Alley.

Without delay, he started for it. But the moment he stepped into the alley, that sixth sense, to which he had more than once been indebted for his life, sounded a subtle warning. Perhaps it was the wolfish eyes that peered at him from the window of the corner pool parlor, the idlers who sauntered out after him.

As he passed the house in which Reef Schneider lived, a low hiss came from the doorway. He turned, and the old man was standing there in the shadows, beckoning frantically.

"Look out!" Reef dared a hoarse whisper. "They're waiting for you! Don't go up—"

From the dark hallway behind him came a sound little more than a cough—the report of a silenced automatic—and Reef Schneider clutched at his throat as he pitched over on his face, his bill for Kentucky Gold settled in full.

Blinky McQuade's eyes blazed behind the hooded spectacles. The loiterers were very close to him now. No mistaking the way their hands were thrust into their coats, the significant pocket bulges trained on him and commanding him to keep moving. Nothing to do but go ahead, turn in at his empty doorway, step across the dimly lit hallway and clump up the creaking stairs. Nothing to do but unlock his door, fling it wide....

But when he leaped across the threshold crouching low and with his body half-turned, his guns were blazing. One surprised killer gaped at him from the middle of the room—and then fell writhing on top of the bed, kicking madly as his hands clutched his belly. The other sent two bullets thudding into the door just above their intended victim's head—then he, too, lost interest as a leaden slug smashed through his temple.

Almost before the fellow's body had thudded to the floor, Blinky McQuade reeled and collapsed in a heap beside him— exactly as the partly opened door of his clothes closet flew back and the automatic muzzle that he had seen covering him, poked out into the room, clutched in the white-knuckled hand of Martin Egelhart!

WARILY, THE assistant district attorney stepped closer and stood over him, the gun trained on his back. Blinky held his breath, expecting to feel hot lead.

"Quit your stalling," Egelhart sneered, prodding McQuade with his foot. "I know you're not dead—and I'm all set for any of your slick tricks. Get up."

Shamefacedly, Blinky got to his feet, standing empty-handed before his captor. The district attorney kicked the relinquished automatics out of reach.

"So, Mr. John A. McQuade," he jeered, "maybe now you wish you'd kept your nose out of things that don't concern you."

But Blinky McQuade wasn't listening to him. All he had heard was that name, John A. McQuade—a name which, he realized suddenly he had used in only one place, Uncle Sam's pawnshop. To everyone else he was known as Blinky.

So it was Egelhart who was behind the pawnshop set-up! It was he who was the master-criminal!

Blinky berated himself scornfully for not having figured that out sooner. The trap set for Mayor Wallace in Great Neck should have told him the truth. If the mayor had been killed at the

Oak Hills Club dance, District Attorney Cunnison, of Queens, would have died with him—and Egelhart would have succeeded his superior in office. Spiegelman would have taken District Attorney Baldwin's place in the New York County office. And, doubtless, there was another conspirator ready to step into the shoes of the Kings County D. A. the moment death had vacated them. At one sweep, Egelhart and his crooked associates would have gotten a strangle-hold on the prosecutors' office.

Egelhart had sprung to the door, closed and locked it against intruders from the hallway. But he did not notice that Blinky had backed up against the wall and edged his way unobtrusively along it while his nervous feet moved restlessly from board to board. When he was directly opposite the open closet he stopped—and suddenly an infernal machine seemed to go off within its depths!

White-faced, Egelhart whirled. Something in that closet was hissing fiercely. There was a muffled explosion.

That was all Egelhart saw before a steely arm whipped around his neck from behind, punishing fingers gripped his gun-wrist and twisted until he howled, dropping his automatic. He was spun around, and Blinky McQuade's fist smashed into his face. Before he could recover, McQuade was in on top of him.

"So you're the murdering devil behind this cowardly reign of terror!"

"I had a part in it!" Egelhart howled. "Yes, I did—but I'm not the one who's responsible. I just followed orders!"

"Who gave the orders?"

"I don't know—I swear I don't know!" the renegade district

attorney mouthed through swelling lips. "I don't know the chief. I've been his right-hand man ever since he trapped me in a bribery deal three months ago. He had evidence against me that I couldn't explain. I had to do what I was told. Since then, I've been getting my orders by telephone or by typewritten messages that suddenly appear on my desk—"

"Written on an Oliver machine?"

Egelhart's eyes widened with surprise.

"I don't know who he is," the attorney returned to his denial.

Perhaps most of that confession was the truth, but the last statement was a lie, and Blinky spotted it at once. Egelhart might have been nothing but the tool he claimed, but his cunning eyes had betrayed his intention of double-crossing his boss and grabbing autocratic power.

"What happened in there?" he nodded toward the closet in which he had been looking curiously.

"Merely a harmless fuse I had attached to a battery in anticipation of a time such as this when it might be needed," Blinky told him. "When the current was turned on the fuse went into action."

"Oh, one of those practical-joke contraptions they attach under the sparkplug of an auto to make the driver think it's going to blow up," Egelhart nodded comprehendingly. "You sure hooked me with it, all right. But what I don't understand is how you managed to set it off."

"Simply by stepping on that board over there against the wall," McQuade answered. His eyes were alert, ready for any trick. The fellow was deliberately stalling, sparring for time; and

Blinky knew it. "There's a button under it that connects with the closet by—"

Police sirens out in the streets stopped his words. That was it—a double-trap. He suddenly realized Egelhart's game. A whistle was shrilling in the hall; heavy-shoed feet were pounding across the pavement in the little courtyard. To be doubly certain that there would be no slip-up; Egelhart had schemed to have the police arrive in time to mop up!

THE ATTORNEY'S eyes gleamed with triumph and he took advantage of McQuade's surprise to make a dash for the door. But before he could turn the key in the lock to admit the police, Blinky seized him by the shoulder, yanked him away, sent him sprawling on the floor—only to come to his knees, a crooked grin on his face, his recovered automatic clutched in his hand!

He fired—and living flame seemed to score Blinky McQuade's ribs as he threw himself forward desperately. Panic stricken, Egelhart tried to trigger the weapon again as he went over backward and was pinned to the floor. But now his wrist was caught in a grip of steel. No matter how frantically he struggled, he could not get away or check his arm from being twisted around and up—pointing the weapon straight at his own head!

"No—no, McQuade! Don't kill me!"

"You're not fit to live!"

The gun in his own fingers roared Martin Egelhart's doom!

Quickly, McQuade recovered his automatics from beneath the bed, slipping them back into their holsters. The police were in the hall, pounding on his door, blocking his way to the roof. They were in the courtyard, cutting him off.

He turned out the gas-light and noiselessly opened one of his windows. The window that was not more than three feet from one in the Pallin Place house that backed at an angle against the one in which he, himself, lived. There was a young girl in that room he knew who generally left her window open.

The window was now open more than a foot. Blinky climbed up onto his windowsill, knelt there, swung out into space. He grabbed the opposite ledge with both hands, then clung with one while he pushed up the window with the other.

Men were shouting up at him. Bullets buzzed around him, as he dragged himself over the sill—to confront a pretty young girl with a hastily donned negligee wrapped around her. But instead of screaming or fainting she thrust a man's topcoat and felt hat into his hands and sprang to open her door. The police, he realized thankfully, haven't many friends in Holy Alley.

The only refuge left open was the penthouse on top of the Hopecrest Apartments. But even that was dangerous.

And yet he had no choice but to go there as quickly as possible. This wound must be fixed up at once.

CHAPTER 10
LOST STAND

WHEN THE door of the sheet-iron hideout garage swung open, the driver at the wheel of the car that emerged was Richard Wentworth—but a Richard Wentworth with face paler than usual.

There seemed to be no police in evidence, as he approached the Hopecrest. None attempted to stop him as he swung into the driveway beside the building, drove to the rear, unlocked the door of the second of a row of garages and halted inside. Wearily, he stepped out of the car and ran his fingers along an edge of the garage floor close to the wall. He pressed the cleverly concealed button that raised a foot-square section of the floor on hinges, like a trapdoor, revealing a recess that contained a make-up kit, a box of emergency tools and a small-sized French telephone.

Wentworth lifted the receiver.

"Everything clear upstairs, Jackson?" he asked tonelessly.

"Everything okay here, sir," the former A.E.F. sergeant reported.

"I'll be right up." Wentworth replaced the phone. Then he operated the trapdoor which opened directly under his car and led, by means of a passageway, to the private self-serviced elevator which connected with the lower floor of the two-story penthouse apartment.

But the men who served him as friends, rather than servants, had not been deceived by his evasion. They were waiting for him when the elevator door opened, their faces filled with concern. Huge, bearded Ram Singh fairly lifted him off his feet and half-carried him to a chair.

"Allah be praised!" he muttered, as he stripped off Wentworth's coat and blood-soaked shirt. "Already there has been much blood lost. A lesser man than the master might not have been able to remain on his feet. But"—as he bathed the wounds with the gentleness of a skilled nurse—"there is no evidence of lasting hurt. A dressing strapped in place and a little rest, and all should mend."

Quickly, Wentworth sketched his visit to Baumann's pawn-shop.

"Kirkpatrick is more than likely to pay us another visit, when Egelhart's body is discovered," he finished. "Have the police been here lately?"

"Not officially, sir," Jackson grinned. "They think we do not even suspect their presence. But I've spotted at least eight of them keeping watch on the block."

"Then they must have seen me drive in," Wentworth mused.

As if in echo of his thought, the telephone rang insistently.

"The police—they're coming in by the dozens!" the switch-board operator in the lower hallway reported excitedly the moment the receiver was off the hook. "They've grabbed the elevators and—"

His voice was chopped off as he was dragged away from the switchboard, and then a voice barked into the mouthpiece.

"Hello, that you, Wentworth?" it demanded. "This is Captain Sinclair. I've got a warrant down here for you, and I'm coming up to serve it."

WENTWORTH HUNG up, and turned thoughtfully to the three old friends who had stood by him so long and faithfully. Already, the Oriental salve the Sikh had worked into his wounds was effecting its magic.

"The police will be up here any minute," he told them. "I

haven't decided just how I'm going to handle this—but I don't want them in here."

The stout steel shutters were already sliding in place, locking outside the bulletproof windows.

Wentworth stood at one of the cleverly concealed peep-holes watching as a wave of blue uniforms poured out of the elevator exits at the other side of the lawn and swarmed over his beautifully landscaped roof-garden. They paused uncertainly when they realized what a fortress confronted them. But only for a moment. Then Sinclair took charge, and a hail of bullets pattered against the shutter.

"They'll soon get tired of that and come back with battering-rams, or maybe even fieldpieces if they have to," Wentworth predicted. "We've got to keep them off. Lay down a gas barrage, Jackson."

In a few moments, the roof was pocked with little puffs of gray smoke that spread and filled the air like a haze. Coughing and choking, the officers fled back to the elevator shaft-house, and the rattle of bullets against the shutters ceased. However, that was but a lull in the storm, Wentworth knew. The police would be back—and gas was the only weapon he could use against them, for, under no circumstances, would he consider returning the fire of these men only doing their duty.

Again the telephone rang, and Jenkyns took the call.

"It's Commissioner Kirkpatrick, sir," he reported doubtfully. "He called me a liar when I said you weren't here—"

Wentworth took the instrument.

"Hello, Dick," Kirkpatrick's voice barked into his ear. "I used to think you had some sense, but now I'm beginning to doubt it. We have a warrant for you, and we're going to serve it—even if we have to blow your castle into little pieces. You're trapped.

"No sense at all in your trying to hold out," Kirkpatrick was saying. "You're just taking those three men of yours to the electric chair with you by endangering my men. So far as you are concerned, I've got the goods on you at last—*Mr. Spider!* That throws a bit of shock into you, eh? And I'm not making wild guesses this time. Peggy Dunning couldn't quite stomach the idea of letting young Morgan go to the chair for a crime you committed, so she came to me and gave me the whole story. She positively identifies you as the Spider and is an eyewitness to your killing of this Joe Ruigi.

Wentworth's eyes snapped with anger as he listened and realized what had happened. Of course, Peggy Dunning did not know he was the Spider, but he could picture her, frantic to save her sweetheart, being pumped and cross-questioned, having her words twisted and others put into her mouth, agreeing to anything that she thought would help Morgan, as Kirkpatrick baited and bulldozed her. That wasn't like Kirk, but this crime wave had him at wit's end.

JENKYNS HAD come back into the room quietly waiting to deliver his report, but Wentworth didn't need to hear it—one look at the old man's worried face was sufficient. Kirk hadn't been bluffing; the elevator was out of commission, and now they were cut off from the garages.

Suddenly, the whole building trembled as a terrific blast

seemed to shake its very foundations. Wordlessly, Wentworth looked at his men. They scattered.

Jackson was first to return, face white.

"That was the garages, sir," he reported. "They've been blown to pieces."

Wentworth nodded, smiling bitterly.

"Been suspicious of you for some time, Dick," Kirkpatrick was still jubilating over the wire, "but I couldn't make myself believe that you had gone insane. That's the only way I can account for this mad scheme of yours to set yourself up as a master of crime too powerful for the law to reach. The trouble with a man who gets a phobia like yours is that he becomes careless and loses his cunning. That's the only reason you put that scarred-hand glove on my hand and stamped your Spider trademark on it. You forgot that the fingerprints on it tie you up with at least a dozen outrages—"

The phone was hardly back in its cradle before the bell began ringing again. Wentworth reached for it—and a different voice greeted him.

"How do you do, Mr. Wentworth?" it chuckled. "Or should I say *Mr. Spider*—or perhaps Mr. John A. McQuade? Well, of what matter the name, anyway? The main thing is that your interference, in all three of your capacities, is at an end. You have caused me considerable trouble—but at last I have run you to your hole. This time there will be no convenient break for you to slip through. Just in case you should find some way to trick the police who are besieging you, it might interest you to know that my men are posted all around your neighborhood. They are ready to take care of you the moment you show your face—or shall I say any one of your three faces?"

The mocking voice was strange, and yet vaguely familiar.

"It was my men who just blew up your ingenious garages—after one of them, who had been waiting where you had your car stored, rode in with you on the spare tire," the caller gloated. "Speaking of explosions, while the police are blasting you out of your hole I think you should know that in the morning the main courtroom in the Criminal Courts Building will be blown to pieces when Slugs Jalnik comes up for sentence. Undoubtedly, that will cause quite a sensation—especially when the police discover that it was Nita van Sloan who did it!"

The receiver clicked at the other end.

Now he knew why Nita had been kidnapped! Now he knew the fiendishly contrived doom that hung over her. And, trapped and helpless on that roof, there was not one thing he could do to stop it!

THE PENTHOUSE was shaking under the terrific bombardment, and the din so deafening that it seemed the place must be coming down around their ears. When he stepped to a window and peered through a peep-hole he saw the police back on the roof in reinforced numbers, equipped now with gas-masks. They had brought up machine guns, and the rattle of lead against the steel shutters was like thunderous quarry-hammers. How long any building could withstand such a pounding was a problem.

Even as that thought flashed through Wentworth's mind, Captain Sinclair lifted a megaphone.

"This is your last warning. Wentworth!" he bellowed. "We're getting bombs! I'm going to blow you out!"

As he stared out at the marked policemen, looking like so many queer beings from another world, an idea flashed into his mind. A desperate idea, but it might work. At least, it should deliver Jackson and Jenkyns and Ram Singh from Kirkpatrick's threat.

Wentworth's lips tightened. Otherwise, his poker-face was inscrutable as he went to a closet and provided himself with a number of coils of rope. He reached into a drawer and grasped a short length of weighted rubber hose....

Ram Singh and Jenkyns were at the windows on the first floor, but Jackson was on guard upstairs when Wentworth came up quietly behind him and brought the bludgeon down over his head. Without a sound, the chauffeur crumpled. Wentworth caught and lowered him gently to the floor. He lashed the man's arms and legs.

"You're going to be mighty sore about this when you wake up, old man," Wentworth muttered, "but you'll understand when you've had a chance to cool off."

When Jackson's body had dropped out of sight, he stepped to the desk, called Ram Singh and asked him to come upstairs. As the Sikh stepped into the room and looked around inquiringly the weighted hose thudded home at the base of his skull. He pitched forward.

"Mighty shabby way to treat a faithful warrior," Wentworth commiserated, tying him up tightly, "but this is the only way I could ever make you agree with what I've got to do." He turned away.

That left only Jenkyns—but he hadn't the heart to handle the old butler so vigorously.

Jenkyns was standing at a peep-hole, nervously watching the latest police assault, when Wentworth's arm wrapped around him and held him helpless. Before the old man knew what was happening, a length of rope pinioned his arms.

"Take it easy, Jenkyns," Wentworth warned. "I'm going to tie you up so that it will look as if you were overcome."

Jenkyns' eyes remained wide, questioning, as his feet were bound together.

"Sorry, Jenkyns, but this is necessary, too." Wentworth forced a gag between his teeth, tied it behind his head. "I'm going to put you just inside the door. I'll leave these ropes around your arms sufficiently loose so that you can edge up to it and slip the lock when I give the signal. I'm counting on you to do that, and then to pretend that you were helpless here all the while this attack was going on. Those are orders, Jenkyns."

When Jenkyns was in position on the floor beside the door, Wentworth released all but one lock, then hurried into a back room. Minutes passed while the walls trembled under the ruinous battering from outside. But even that tumult was dwarfed by a new, terrific explosion.

Pictures dropped from the walls; vases danced and fell from their pedestals; bits of plaster rained down from the ceiling. Jenkyns' agonized eyes turned to where a cloud of dust was billowing through the rear doorway. Like a martyr going to the stake, he propped himself up on one elbow, drew the last bolt, turned the knob and tugged at the door....

In a blue-crested wave the police charged through that doorway. For a moment, they hesitated just across the threshold. Then the clouds of dust drew them like a magnet to the back room—a room an utter wreck. Broken furniture lay shattered against the walls, as if a gigantic broom had swept it out of the way—and under the overturned ruin of a couch lay what seemed to be a torn, bleeding body!

Almost reverently, they lifted the debris and stared down at the mangled horror—until Captain Sinclair suddenly bent down suspiciously.

"This is a fake!" he whirled on his men. "It's nothing but a paint-smeared dummy!"

His voice gagged in his throat as one of his subordinates yelled in surprise and pointed out of an unshuttered window on the sheer, street side of the building. There, floating in the air like a huge umbrella was an unfurled parachute with the figure of a man clinging to it!

"Get him!" Sinclair howled, grabbing a Tommy-gun.

His profane description of Richard Wentworth was drowned by the roar of half a dozen machine guns. In mid-flight, those streams of lead caught the parachute, riddled it, swept lower and tore into the swaying body. Wildly, its legs danced in the air—then it plummeted downward as the torn parachute collapsed.

With one accord like a horde of gargoyle-faced mercenaries, Sinclair's men bolted and raced across the gas-reeking terrace.

Quickly, the packed elevators shot them down to the ground floor. They surged into the street.

One of those gas-masked runners was slower than the rest. He lagged behind, and then ran a block farther than the others before he hailed a taxicab and barked the address of Sam Baumann's pawnshop to the startled driver. He flung himself inside, ripped the suffocating mask from his face—to reveal the features of Richard Wentworth!

WENTWORTH HAD been mentally reviewing his conversation with the gloating crime dictator. Only the pawn-shop keeper knew Blinky's name as John A. McQuade, now that Martin Egelhart was dead. That meant that the Bowery shop must be the master-criminal's hideout, and Sam Baumann his tool until he had turned on the old man....

The store was dark and apparently deserted when he got out of the cab on the opposite corner. The door was locked, but, when he made his way to the back yard, he found that only a pasteboard covering had been tucked into the broken lavatory window. It was the work of a minute to tear it loose, climb through.

Sam Baumann's room behind the shop was empty, the floor still stained with his blood. Stillness held in the place, broken only by the occasional rumble of a passing elevated train. Then Wentworth caught a sound that seemed to come from somewhere beneath him. Someone was speaking.

Cautiously, he prowled through the junk-piled rooms until he located a stairs that led to the cellar. The sound of that chuckling voice grew louder. At the far end he found another stairs that led down into a bottomless pit.

Noiselessly, he tiptoed to the doorway—then grunted in amazement. Two shabbily dressed old crones were the sub-cellar room's only occupants. One was busily at work at a table, while the other sat stiffly on a backless stool, apparently dazed. Something about her wrinkled face held Wentworth's attention—until he saw what her companion was doing.

Fascinated, he watched the old woman stuff the fingers of one of those familiar scarred-hand gloves with various materials and wire them to the clocklike arrangement zippered in place in the palm of the hand. Nitro-glycerin was going into that glove—enough to cause a fearful explosion! As soon as that was filled, she started on another—glove after glove piled in on top of those that already half-filled a scrub-pail standing beside her!

"Eleven o'clock," she chuckled as she set the timing gear on one of them. "Eleven o'clock tomorrow morning, when Judge Norton will be right in the middle of his virtuous lecture to Slugs Jalnik. He's going to finish that lecture in hell!"

With a taunting laugh she grabbed up half a dozen of the empty gloves and turned to her companion. She tore open the neck of the dazed woman's dress and stuffed the gloves down into her bosom.

"That's just so there will be no mistake when the police pick up your body," she mocked. "It would be a shame not to have you get full credit for such an artistic job. Some of these gloves I've filled are duds. They won't go off, but will be found nailed to the bottoms of the courtroom benches when the wreckers clean up the debris. That will tell the clever police just how the trick was worked. When they find the others there in your dress, they'll know the story."

Wentworth stared again at that sitting woman. He saw that she was literally frozen with horror. Her brain seemed numbed. Only her wide eyes, blazing out of her lined, grayish-white face, betrayed her torment. That make-up and outfit were perfect. They had transformed her into one of the army of scrubwomen who toil while the city sleeps—*but beneath them Nita van Sloan quaked!*

"That's about all," her companion announced, as she arranged a scrub-rag over the contents of her pail so that the deadly gloves were completely concealed. "Pick up your bucket. We've got a lot of work to do before morning. Put these hammers and nails in yours. I'll carry the 'eggs.' Remember, the first time you pull anything you'll get another needle."

Nita, helpless in the hands of this fiendish harridan! Richard Wentworth's blood was like an icy jelly in his veins as he tensed himself. But before he could move Nita was ahead of him. Frantic-eyed, she lunged for her companion's pail, snatched up one of those infernal gloves, swept it up over her head—

There was sufficient high explosive in that glove to blow the sub-cellar to pieces!

Somehow, Wentworth got his fingers on the thing, juggled it perilously for a moment that seemed an eternity, and then clutched it firmly. Weak-kneed, perspiration-soaked, he turned to lay it on the table—just as the snarling crone leaped.

FOR A moment, the vicious fury of her attack bore him to the ground. Then red rage rioted through him that made him forget that she was a woman or anything except a murderous criminal. He got his fingers on her throat, battered her head down against the floor. He smashed that head until the whole top seemed to be coming off! The gray wig dropped to the floor and completed Wentworth's startled identification of old Uncle Sam Baumann!

"All right—all right. You needn't kill me!" the pawnshop keeper struggled.

Warily, Wentworth backed away, and, at gun-muzzle, herded him a safe distance from that pail of sudden death.

"You're surprised at my identity, of course," he grinned. "I can't say as much for myself. You have a reputation for being very baffling and elusive, my dear Spider, but I found it quite simple to identify you. The day you took such an interest in Miss van Sloan's brooch was a bad give-away. That made me investigate Blinky McQuade. I tied him up immediately with Richard Wentworth, Miss van Sloan's adventurous fiancé. The Spider had already taken a hand in my affairs when he interrupted proceedings in the Dunning home. And, when Miss van Sloan took such an interest in Peggy Dunning, I had another angle on your triple character. When the Spider came to Blinky McQuade's rescue so opportunely at the Bit House, the trinity interlocked beautifully."

"Very interesting," Wentworth nodded, "but just at present I am more interested in unscrambling those personalities. That can be done by a confession from you."

With the automatic muzzle pressed against the back of his

neck, Baumann went to the table, found a sheet of paper, fished a stub of pencil out and stuck it in his mouth to wet the point.

"Not so good as an Oliver—but it will do," he grinned.

"A full confession of your responsibility for the criminal reign of terror of the past few weeks," Wentworth ordered. "A clear statement that the Spider was in no way involved with you," as the stub of pencil laboriously traveled over the paper. "And now a detailed account of your relations with Joe Ruigi, and why he went out to the Dunning house—so that Ed Morgan will be cleared of murder."

Obediently, Bauman scribbled, while the pencil stub went back and forth to his lips. As he reached the end of the page, his hand became slow, uncertain—and, when he finished signing his name, the pencil propped from his fingers.

Wentworth saw that his face had drained of all color, his legs doubling up.

"Too late—can't do anything now," he gasped. "The lead in that pencil—filled with deadly poison—"

He was dying.

"It always ends this way," he shook his head reprovingly. "Stealing—killing—the wages of sin, my boy—"

Richard Wentworth left the confession on the table beneath the pail of bombs. For a moment, he bent over the still figure, and the bottom of his cigarette lighter pressed against Sam Baumann's forehead. It left the crimson mark of the Spider on the brow of the would-be lord of the underworld, grim warning to any who might be tempted to step into his shoes!

THOUGHTFULLY, WENTWORTH walked upstairs

with Nita, but, before they left the dark pawnshop, he stepped to the telephone and called Kirkpatrick.

"Hello, Kirk," he greeted, and knew at once that Kirkpatrick had recognized his voice. "No—don't bother to put a tracer on this call. I'm going to give you the address, and I'll be gone before you can get here. Better get here as soon as you can, though. There's something down in the sub-cellar that will interest you.

"After you've had a look around here, I think you'll want to forget that made-to-order testimony you dragged out of Peggy Dunning. Probably, you'll be coming around to apologize to me. But I won't see you for a while, Kirk. Nita and I are going away—to see if we can find a friend who will appreciate it when we put our necks in the noose to pull his bacon out of the fire."

Bitter words—but the warmth in the voice told Kirkpatrick that they were not as bitter as they sounded; Richard Wentworth forgave his panic-bred blunders.